FELICITY GREEN

THE
WITCH CLUB
A SCOTTISH WITCHES MYSTERY

CHAPTER ONE

ANDIE

The boat glided across the lake as if it floated on the dense fog. The tall woman at the bow resembled a figurehead: wooden posture, chin high, gaze fixed ahead.

The loch could have been any lake in the Scottish Highlands, but Andie knew, like you know things in dreams, that it was Loch Lomond.

When they reached the shore, the woman with the shoulder-length dark blond hair stepped off the boat. Andie recognized her. It was Dessie McKendrick.

Dessie turned to face her. By now, Andie was sure what kind of dream this was, because she, herself, was present in it. She followed Dessie to the cluster of houses close to the shore. It was Tarbet, Andie's hometown. Andie recognized the B&B signs. Every second house in Tarbet rented out guest rooms. The picturesque village in the Highlands lived off tourism.

Dessie was also at home in Tarbet. Having moved here a few years ago, Dessie too was the owner of a B&B. That appeared to be her destination now, in Andie's dream. Dessie kept looking over her shoulder to make sure Andie was following her. Her gray eyes showed no emotion, yet her body language screamed tension.

Dessie's B&B was a whitewashed, sprawling cottage that Andie had never entered before. She followed Dessie into the house until they were standing in front of door number three. Dessie looked at Andie, paused for a moment, then took a set of keys from her pocket and unlocked the door. Suddenly, Andie found herself in the middle of the room with no recollection of having entered. The door was closed.

Dessie, or to be more precise, Dessie's double, slowly raised her index finger and placed it on her lips. Andie looked around the room. The walls were full of newspaper clippings, photos, and documents. She could spot the floral wallpaper peeking from behind the collage in places, but most of the wall space was covered. Countless items were strewn about the floor.

Beneath the chaos, Andie could make out an ordinary guest room. That had probably been its original function. A large desk was squeezed into a corner. The doors to the closet, overstuffed with men's clothing, were open. On the floor, items were piled in small heaps; a tower of CDs here, a stack of books there. In one corner stood a collection of dusty whisky bottles on a stainless-steel cart. In front of the bed was a large green backpack and other camping gear. A few more unusual items were spread out on the bed. At first glance, Andie had thought it was clutter, but now she saw the items had been sorted by size. A silver letter opener, a music box with circus animals, small modern art prints, a dartboard, pool cues.

Dessie's double took the music box in her hand, then put it down again. She walked to the wall, pointed to a photo, and twisted her mouth into a smile that didn't reach her eyes.

The photo showed a young man who looked attractive

in a Californian surfer kind of way. Bright blue eyes, tousled blond hair, dazzling white teeth, tanned. Dessie still seemed somehow mechanical, as was typical for doubles. But tears were flowing from her expressionless eyes, rolling down her pale cheeks.

Andie waited anxiously to see what would happen next. Maybe this really was just a dream. She hoped so. But deep inside, she knew what would happen in the end. This wasn't her first rodeo.

Dessie's skin became paler and drier until it resembled parchment paper. Andie tried to wake up. It didn't work. Dream-Andie remained frozen on the spot as Dessie's gray eyes receded into their sockets, her hair fell out in clumps, and the nails detached from her fingers. The tall woman shriveled before Andie's eyes, turning into a mummy.

Andie recognized all too well the feeling of helplessness that now overcame her. Again, she tried hard to awaken, but Dream-Andie didn't even manage to avert her eyes. She was forced to watch Dessie McKendrick disintegrate.

Then came the worst, the thing that had always scared Andie when she'd been younger. Little white maggots spilled from Dessie's orifices: the eye sockets, the ears, the mouth, the nostrils. The worms appeared to consume her from the inside, leaving only bones and the parchment of skin. Finally, the bone-skin structure also collapsed. Beetles and other insects appeared out of nowhere, feasting on the remains of Dessie McKendrick. The tiny pile on the wooden floorboards in room number three that had once been Dessie disappeared faster than Andie could feel repulsed by the spectacle.

From experience, Andie knew there was no point in trying to wake herself up. She had to watch the whole process to the end.

When Dessie was fully gone, the room turned cold. Dream-Andie's teeth chattered. She wrapped her arms

5

around her shivering body. Mist drifted into the room from under the door, through the open window, and from various cracks and crevices in the walls. Soon the entire room was full of dense fog, like the one that clung to the loch, so that Andie could no longer see anything. Panicked, she tried to remember which direction the exit was.

She had to escape this dream. This house. This room.

Desperately, Andie groped for the door and got hold of a knob. When she opened her eyes, it took her a moment to realize that she was standing in her room in Edinburgh. She was no longer dreaming; she was awake, and she was sleepwalking. It was her door, her door handle, not the one in room number three in Dessie's B&B. Her breath came fast, and she was freezing.

It took her a while to trust the feeling of relief. She grabbed her robe from the hook on the back of the door and pulled it on. The room in the house she shared with other students was bathed in pale moonlight. Andie sat down on the edge of her bed, turned on the bedside lamp, and tried to remember everything about the dream.

Visions like that hadn't plagued her since she'd started her biotechnology studies here in Edinburgh. She had been quite happy to escape Tarbet, although she had always known that her special gift would probably take her back.

Even to a quiet, introverted girl like her, the village seemed boring. Edinburgh was a lot more exciting. And she had options. She didn't have to make herself small. Still, she had to work hard to succeed, and not just academically. She also had to take on jobs to finance her studies. Her parents weren't exactly well off. The spring term had just ended, and Andie had to find full-time employment, anyway. This new revelation had dashed her hope of spending the summer break in Edinburgh.

Of course, there was always the option of ignoring the dream. But she didn't dare, and not just because she was a conscientious person. She knew by experience that if she suppressed her visions they would only get worse, and a consuming darkness would grow inside her. She would no longer be able to sleep, eat, or leave her room—until she responded to the double's cry for help.

Dessie McKendrick needed her—and she probably didn't even know it.

Andie's friend Tara usually worked at Dessie's B&B over the summer. Maybe Andie could take her place. Tara would understand the special circumstances.

Andie pushed a strand of her long, dark brown hair behind her ear and sighed. Then she got up, pulled her suitcase out of the closet, and started packing. Tomorrow morning, she would leave for Tarbet. There was no reason to put it off.

She had a calling to answer.

CHAPTER TWO

DESSIE

G rayson pointed to the bottle of wine. Dessie just shook her head, picked up her empty glass, and went to the counter at the other end of the large kitchen/breakfast room. She placed the glass in the sink. When she didn't hear wine being poured from the bottle, her shoulders relaxed a fraction.

She couldn't afford to have more than one drink with Grayson. She had enjoyed the conversation as much as ever but now wished Grayson would retire to his room. Still, she was a little disappointed when she heard the scraping of the chair.

Raindrops pattered softly against the window above the sink. A typical Scottish summer. One reason she loved living here, Dessie thought bitterly.

Grayson cleared his throat. "I'd better get some sleep. An early start for me tomorrow."

"Oh, right, your trip," Dessie said, still staring out the window into the dark and rainy night. The thought of missing Grayson made Dessie uncomfortable. She tried to ignore the kaleidoscope of butterflies in her stomach that seemed to get bigger every year, ever since the American businessman had become a permanent summer season guest at Dessie's B&B.

For a long time, Dessie had resisted the development of a friendship. But eventually small talk had turned into deeper conversations. Now they had gotten into the habit of ending the evening with a shared bottle of wine in the large room.

Of course, Dessie felt guilty. But there was another emotion, something delicious, dangerous, that she couldn't entirely ignore. Obviously, there was no way she would act upon it.

Dessie turned to face Grayson. She didn't have to force a smile as she looked at the handsome man with clear blue eyes and dark hair. His gray temples made him look older than he was, probably in his late thirties or early forties. They also gave him an air of respectability that could only benefit him in his work as a financial advisor.

At least, that's what Dessie thought his profession was. He was a little vague about the exact nature of his business. All she knew was that he had to be rather successful. After all, he could afford to take extended summer vacations every year. But sometimes he met with clients in Europe during this time, like the business trip to Paris tomorrow.

Dessie had to bite her tongue so she wouldn't accidentally let slip that she'd miss him. It was safer to say nothing at all. This wouldn't offend Grayson; he had to be used to her distant demeanor by now. He quietly wished her a good night, gave her a bright smile, and then went to his room.

Dessie took Grayson's glass, finished the last sip he always left—a habit of his—and put it next to hers in the sink. She toyed with the idea of not doing the washing up but quickly changed her mind. It would add to her long list of chores in the morning, and it might stress her out.

Dessie didn't like to switch up her routine, as it sometimes was the only thing that got her through her day.

She was about to turn on the faucet when the doorbell rang. Dessie looked at the clock above the door. Her brows drew together.

The water taxi from the hostel, she thought, and an icy shiver ran down her spine. When guests arrived this late, it was usually West Highland Way hikers who couldn't get a room at the Rowardennan Youth Hostel across the loch. A queasy feeling took hold of Dessie as she walked to the front door.

When she opened it, she saw four young people with large backpacks. Dessie turned on the outside light. Two women and two men in their early twenties, soaked from the rain, stared back at her.

"How can I help?" Dessie asked.

"Your sign doesn't say No Vacancies," one of the young women whined. Her red curls were stuck to her face, black mascara had left marks on her cheeks, and her lipstick was smudged. Dessie couldn't muster much sympathy for her. Just another example of hikers who had underestimated the strenuousness of the famous long-distance trail from Milngavie near Glasgow to Fort William in the Highlands. This young woman, who was probably lugging a large make-up kit in her backpack, would most definitely not make it to Fort William. At least not on foot. Dessie suspected the girl and her friends would catch the West Highland Railway tomorrow and cut the nine-day hike short.

"Please tell us you still have rooms available." The young woman looked at her with big blue doll's eyes.

"I only have one queen room left," Dessie said, shrugging her shoulders apologetically. She was about to close the door when Red slid a foot in. She was halfway through the entrance before Dessie could do anything about it.

"We'll take it," she yelled, grabbing the young man standing next to her by the wrist and pulling him into the house.

"One room with a queen-size bed," Dessie repeated, taken somewhat off guard. "So not enough room for four people, I'm afraid."

"You're our last resort," said the woman, brushing the wet hair out of her face. "We've been everywhere, but there are no vacancies in this whole effing place."

"But Val," said the young man, still attached to the redhead. "What about Nicole and Nate? We can't just—"

"Well, first come, first served," Val cut him off. "Do we all have to suffer and stand in the rain just because there's only one room left?" She let go of the young man and shrugged off her backpack. "I swear, this damn thing gets heavier by the minute!"

"I'm sorry," the very average-looking man said in the direction of the other young woman.

The petite brunette with big sad eyes still standing outside the door pulled up the hood of her raincoat. "It's okay, Sam." She sounded resigned. Then she turned to her companion, who stood a little further back. He just looked down at his shoes and mumbled unintelligibly.

"Do you have any advice where they could go?" Sam turned to Dessie.

The hairs on the back of her neck stood up, and she could hardly breathe. Without blinking, she stared at the young man for what felt like an eternity.

He looked uncertain. "Excuse me, but do you know if there are any vacancies in the area?" Sam repeated his question, probably assuming she had not understood him.

Dessie swallowed hard, took a deep breath, and cleared her throat. She had to pull herself together. Don't be daft, she scolded herself.

She forced herself to say the words, even though it was

hard to get them out. "I'm sure Mrs. MacDonald has a room available. Two streets up the hill on the left. It's called the Thistle Inn, but it's actually..." Dessie trailed off.

"Why don't you try that," Sam said to the others. "Or maybe we should all go there...?"

He looked at Val. She shook her head. "We're staying here," she decided.

"Inn is a little misleading," Dessie continued. "It's just two guest rooms in Mrs. MacDonald's house. You'd share the bathroom with her. It's kind of a traditional B&B, if you know what I mean. Maybe you young people wouldn't like to stay in such an, uh, old-fashioned place," she added hopefully.

But it didn't help. After all, this was a last refuge for the unlikely hikers. A roof over their heads was better than standing in the rain, even if it was the worst B&B in Tarbet. Well, it wasn't exactly bad, but... Dessie shook her head as if she could shake off her gloomy thoughts.

The young woman with the big eyes looked back at the other man, whose face Dessie could not make out in the dark and the rain. "So...shall we?"

Nate shrugged indecisively and mumbled something that sounded like, "I don't care."

"Well then." Nicole sighed and waved goodbye to the other two. "See you tomorrow."

"Room number five," Dessie said tonelessly to Val and Sam. The two continued into the house, but Dessie stayed at the door for a moment watching the sad figures, one tall, one short, disappear into the dark night.

She knew it was completely irrational, but she couldn't shake the horrible feeling that she had sent Nate and Nicole to their doom.

CHAPTER THREE

ANDIE

ndie MacLeod stifled a yawn as she unlocked the door to Dessie's B&B at half past six the next morning. They served breakfast from seven to nine and then had to clean and get rooms ready for new guests. Andie wasn't an early riser, but it was nice to finish work by noon most days.

Sometimes she had to return to the B&B later in the afternoon to check in guests on the days Dessie wasn't there, but most of the time her boss ran errands at midday, when the B&B was closed. Dessie seemed to live a very quiet life, staying in most evenings. As far as Andie knew, she didn't have any close friends or hobbies to speak of. In the village, she was known as a recluse; an outsider still, after ten years of living here.

Andie walked into the B&B and saw Dessie standing in the corridor. She wanted to wish her a good morning, but the words kind of got stuck in her throat when she noticed her boss's expression. Dessie's gray eyes looked enormous in her gaunt face. Her cheeks were flushed. She had one hand at her throat, as if she couldn't breathe.

Taken aback, Andie stopped in her tracks. Dessie didn't greet her. She pulled a bundle of keys from her pocket, but it slipped through her fingers. Dessie stared at the keys on the floor for a few seconds before bending down and picking them up. She unlocked the door to room number three and disappeared inside. Andie stood there and listened to the key turning from the inside.

As odd as it seemed, Dessie's behavior wasn't unusual. Andie had seen Dessie go into this room several times before. Her boss had explained to her they did not assign number three to any guest; it was for her own private use. Dessie had the only key, and nobody was allowed to go inside.

Tara had already briefed Andie about Dessie's eccentric behavior regarding this room. With a giggle, she had made several guesses as to what the woman might be hiding in there. Dead bodies? Leather fetish stuff? Exotic animals? An action figure collection?

Andie, who knew what the room looked like from the inside, hadn't wanted to share her information with Tara. She'd suggested that it might be a sacred space, like a meditation room.

Obviously, Tara knew about Andie's special talent. They had grown up together, were the same age, and had been classmates, but despite these common grounds, they couldn't have been more different. Andie didn't really like the superficial girl who was mainly interested in make-up, clothes, and boys.

Despite Andie's insider information, she was dying to find out what room number three looked like in real life. It would reveal itself to her eventually, she thought to herself, as she walked toward the kitchen.

Dessie was clearly upset, but her boss didn't strike her as the kind of person who would appreciate it if Andie tried to get her to talk about her troubles. Andie had only been working here for a couple of weeks, after all. She decided the best thing to do in this situation would be to keep her head down and do her work. She'd just go ahead and prepare breakfast, like any other day.

To Andie's surprise, there were already two guests waiting in the breakfast room: a red-haired young woman and a tall young man. They had to be about Andie's age.

They must have noticed Andie's raised eyebrows because they came over and introduced themselves. "Hi, we're Val and Sam," the young man said.

Andie walked to the cabinet, took out plates, and started setting the tables. "I'm Andie, I work here. Did you know we don't serve breakfast until seven?"

The two looked at each other. "Yes, we know," the redhead said. "But we were hoping we could get something sooner. A cup of coffee? A slice of toast?"

Andie noticed Sam shifting from one foot to the other. Val, too, looked nervous.

"Why don't you take a seat?" Andie said with what she hoped was a reassuring tone of voice.

"We might have upset the owner with our question," Sam said. "She dropped the glasses she was going to put in the cabinet over there and ran off."

"We don't want to put anyone out, but a cup of coffee isn't too much of an ask, is it?" Val said.

With a furrowed brow, Andie walked over to the cabinet. That's when she noticed the broken wine glasses on the floor. "Um, yes…I mean, no. I'll turn on the machine in a sec," Andie said absentmindedly.

"As we've already explained to the owner," Sam continued, "our friend Nicole called earlier. She and her boyfriend, Nate, stayed at the Thistle Inn last night. There was only one room available here, and they had to find a different place to stay. Well, and now…now Nate seems to have disappeared, or something like that."

"Anyway, Nicole called at the crack of dawn, totally panicked." Val seemed compelled to explain, probably because she hoped Andie would stop standing around and start making breakfast already. "When she woke up this morning, Nate wasn't there. She asked us to come over as fast as we can. I'm not sure what she wants us to do there, exactly. Us holding her hand won't make him return any faster. He'll probably be back by the time we get there."

Lost in thought, Andie turned on the coffee maker and took out the bread. "The Thistle Inn? Mrs. MacDonald?"

"Yes, that's right." Val sat down at a table. "Nate probably just went for a walk. He gets these weird notions. Maybe he wanted to see the Arrochar Alps at sunrise or whatever."

"Without letting Nicole know?" Sam was still standing. He pulled his phone out of his pocket. "She hasn't texted to say he's back yet, and it's been at least an hour since she noticed him missing."

Val waved her hand dismissively, visibly annoyed. She lightened up when Andie handed her a cup of coffee. "Can you stop worrying about it until after we've had breakfast?" She took a sip.

Andie put a couple of slices of bread in the large toaster and placed a selection of jams and honey on Val's table. "How about some eggs and bacon? That should be quick."

She didn't wait for an answer and took the large skillet out of the cupboard. Most of the other guests were bound to ask for the hearty full Scottish fry-up. If she had to cook breakfast orders by herself, it could get stressful fast. It sure was strange, even for Dessie, to leave her guests here by themselves without giving them any answers.

Val interrupted Andie's thoughts with an answer to her earlier question. "Gross, no, I don't do bacon."

"Then nothing for me, either," Sam said.

Andie quickly set up cereal boxes, fruit, milk, and juices at the breakfast buffet, then grabbed a broom and dustpan and cleaned up the broken glass. "Um, did I understand you correctly, earlier? Dessie, I mean Mrs. McKendrick, just ran out of the room when you asked for breakfast?"

"Well, not right away," Val replied with her mouth full, swallowing her bite before continuing. "It wasn't until we explained why we'd like to have breakfast early that she dropped the glasses. I thought she was going to get a broom or something, but when she didn't come back..." Val shrugged.

"I guess it reminded her of her own past," Andie thought out loud. When she turned around, Sam and Val were looking at her expectantly. Andie blushed. "Dessie's husband disappeared ten years ago," she continued, annoyed that she had put herself in this position. She hoped she'd get away with this brief explanation.

No such luck. She had just made them more interested.

"What do you mean, disappeared?" Val wanted to know. "Is he still missing?"

"Yes," Andie muttered, turning her back to the pair and busying herself with preparations for the Scottish fry-up, which typically consisted of eggs, bacon, black pudding, sausages, mushrooms, tomatoes, and hash browns.

"Did he disappear from this B&B?" Val asked again.

"No, Dessie didn't own the B&B then. She didn't even live here yet. Dessie and her husband were tourists, like you, spending a night here in Tarbet. Then her husband disappeared, and... That's all I know," Andie said, biting her lip.

"But—" Val wouldn't quit.

17

"It's been ten years," Andie interrupted. She forced herself to smile and turned around. "I was only a kid when it happened."

Val turned her attention to Sam, who seemed most concerned with his phone. "Jesus, I'm sure you won't miss a text alert." She rolled her eyes in annoyance. "Besides, I'm sure she'll call when Nate shows up again."

"*If* he shows up again," Sam said skeptically, still staring at the display.

Andie went back to cutting mushrooms but watched Val and Sam out of the corner of her eye. The young man's disappearance was odd, especially considering the parallels to what had happened to Dessie ten years ago. But Andie had never seen Val and Sam before, in dreams or otherwise, and she was pretty sure that her assignment here had nothing to do with them. She would have known before anyone else if something bad had happened to Nate. She felt pretty confident when she agreed with Val. "I'm sure this Nate will turn up soon."

"I don't think so." Dessie's voice sounded calm. Andie hadn't been aware that her boss had come back into the kitchen.

She turned to face her. Dessie's expression seemed completely neutral again, as if nothing unusual had ever happened. "I'm pretty certain Nate won't be coming back."

She walked over to Val and Sam's table. In a tone they couldn't refuse, she said, "Come on, let's pick up Nicole and drive to the Helensburgh police station."

Val and Sam looked at each other, a little unsure at first, but they both stood up.

"Um, okay," Val said. But Dessie had already stormed out of the room. Val and Sam followed her. Andie watched through the window as they got into Dessie's car.

She chewed her lower lip, then looked at the clock. Five

minutes to seven. Luckily, the other guests seemed to be in no hurry this morning. She had enough time to make a phone call. Andie pulled her phone out of her pocket and dialed a number she had on speed dial: Mrs. MacDonald at the Thistle Inn.

CHAPTER FOUR

DESSIE

I t was a thirty-minute drive to the Helensburgh police station, but it felt like an eternity to everyone in the car. Val, riding shotgun, had started off with questions for Dessie. Was it really necessary to involve the police? But Dessie had answered only in monosyllables. Nicole, whom they had picked up at the Thistle Inn, was just biting her fingernails. Her eyes, which Dessie met in the rearview mirror from time to time, seemed even sadder than last night. Sam kept looking at Nicole with concern. Val, visibly annoyed, had her arms folded in front of her chest, staring sullenly out the window.

Dessie couldn't imagine that Val was that upset about not continuing the hike. She suspected that the red-haired young woman wasn't pleased about someone else being at the center of attention for once.

The oppressive silence in the car became increasingly uncomfortable the closer they got to Helensburgh. Dessie felt great relief when she finally made the turn into the parking lot in front of the police station.

"Now wait a minute!" Val called after her, as they

headed inside. "I want to know what makes you so sure that we have to report Nate missing."

"He still hasn't returned," Nicole said in a soft voice, holding up her phone. "Mrs. MacDonald promised she'd call if he did."

Val sighed in exasperation. "He's bound to come back. Let's not make an unnecessary fuss about this."

"He wouldn't have let Nicole worry," Sam put in. "What if he had an accident or…"

Dessie didn't hear him finish that sentence because she was already through the revolving doors of the police building.

At the front desk sat a lady who at first glance looked like a homely Scottish grandmother, gray hair piled into a loose bun, glasses perched low on the tip of her nose. It would have fit the picture if she'd busied herself with a pair of knitting needles in between answering calls. But as Dessie stepped closer, she realized first impressions could be deceiving.

The receptionist, Rosa Simmonds according to her name tag, had very sharp eyes. Her voice matched her appearance, though, Dessie thought, as she said softly in a throaty Highland accent, "Wylcome, ma dearie. How can I help?"

"I really need to talk to Inspector Murray," Dessie replied in a rather gruff tone. She didn't have time for the usual small talk.

"I've got bad news for you there…Miss McKendrick, is it? Inspector Murray retired two years ago. What's this about?"

"Mrs. McKendrick," Dessie corrected her. "I'd rather discuss that with the Detective Inspector in charge, if it's all the same to you."

"Thought I'd recognized you." Rosa chatted on

nonchalantly. "You are the owner of Dessie's B&B, am I right?"

"Yes, yes. So who is Inspector Murray's successor?"

"That would be Inspector Declan Reid, dearie. Why don't you tell me what's the matter and we'll see who can best help you?"

In the meantime, Sam, Nicole, and Val had also made it into the reception area. Rosa gave them a curious look.

"Nicole's boyfriend, Nate, has disappeared," Dessie said, sighing. "However, I need to speak with Inspector Reid first. I have information he needs to know."

"Oh, poor lamb," Rosa addressed Nicole. "How long has he been——"

"Listen," Dessie interrupted. "It's of vital importance that I talk to Inspector Reid right away."

Rosa looked at her critically over the rim of her glasses.

"All right, now, dinna fash. Let me see what I can do."

Rosa disappeared through the door that led to the interior of the police headquarters. The wall behind Rosa's desk was made of glass, though the middle strip was frosted, and you couldn't see what was happening on the other side. Dessie, who luckily was quite tall, remedied that by standing on her tiptoes, which just about enabled her to peer into the open-plan office.

She spotted Rosa talking to a young man who wasn't dressed in uniform as most of the others were. Instead, he wore an ill-fitting suit. During his conversation with Rosa, he grabbed the knot of his tie and loosened it.

Dessie squinted her eyes a little to make out Inspector Reid's features. He was young. At least, not much older than Dessie herself, so in his early to midthirties. His brown hair was a bit too long, and judging by the tousled look, he was probably in the habit of running his hands through it regularly.

Suddenly, Rosa and Inspector Reid turned their heads

in Dessie's direction. Blushing, she quickly ducked. She'd made it back in front of Rosa's desk when the receptionist opened the door. "Please come in, Mrs. McKendrick."

Dessie rushed past her and plopped down on the chair in front of Inspector Reid's desk. "Inspector," she said, a little out of breath, "my name is Dessie McKendrick. I'm the owner of a B&B in Tarbet, and I've lived there for about ten years, ever since my husband disappeared. And that's precisely the reason I need to talk to you..."

"Slow down, Mrs. McKendrick," Inspector Reid interrupted her. His authoritative tone didn't quite match his disheveled appearance—or the hint of uncertainty in his light brown eyes. "I'm aware of your situation. Rosa has informed me of what happened to your husband. There is no need to get into that right now. I understand this is about someone else who has gone missing?"

"Yes, but I fear it's directly related to what happened to my husband," Dessie replied gruffly. She was annoyed that she once again faced a police officer who dismissed her concerns. She had dared to hope that the new inspector would be more competent than his predecessor, the condescending Inspector Murray. But her hopes had already been dashed. She would just have to explain everything in great detail. Dessie sighed and started again. "Now, just listen to me, please."

DI Reid sat back and motioned for her to continue.

"Exactly ten years ago this summer, my husband Connor and I spent the night in Tarbet. We had just gotten married and were spending our honeymoon in the Highlands. My husband is...was from Edinburgh, and I was a student at the University of Kent. We hiked the West Highland Way and ended up making a detour to Tarbet. We arrived there late in the evening, and despite the many B&Bs and inns, there was no room vacant anywhere. Finally, we were told to try Mrs. MacDonald's Thistle Inn.

As it happened, the two rooms at the Thistle Inn weren't occupied, and we rented one for the night."

Dessie took a deep breath, and Inspector Reid looked pointedly at his wristwatch. Dessie's anger at his behavior worked to balance out the shock and sadness that usually paralyzed her, even ten years later, as she recounted what had happened next.

"When I woke up the next morning, Connor was gone. And, to make a long story short, he remains missing to this day. The investigation was dropped pretty quickly because your predecessor..." Dessie waved her arms in agitation. "Inspector Murray didn't think that Connor's disappearance was a case for the police. Maybe you can guess why he didn't take the situation seriously. A young man, no history of mental illness, no sign of violence or third-party interference...the conclusion was that he left voluntarily. Inspector Murray thought Connor's financial situation was odd, and there were other inconsistencies..." Dessie realized she'd been talking herself into a frenzy and forced herself to calm down. "But that doesn't matter now. The fact is, I have been the only one trying to solve this case, sadly unsuccessfully, and my husband's disappearance remains unexplained to this day. Now, Inspector Reid, you *must* resume the investigation!"

"I must?" DI Reid raised his eyebrows.

"Yes!" Dessie cried impatiently. "Don't you understand? The very same thing has happened again! A young man has disappeared, almost exactly ten years later, from the Thistle Inn. Mrs. MacDonald is involved again. Surely, that can't be a coincidence."

Inspector Reid shifted uncomfortably in his chair. "Now, wait a minute, we don't know if..."

"Yesterday evening, two young couples stood outside my door. We had only one room left, apparently the only one vacant in all of Tarbet. One couple took the room; the other was left standing in the rain. I had no choice but to send them to the Thistle Inn. After all, I didn't want them to wander around Tarbet all night. I knew the chances were good that Mrs. MacDonald's rooms were unoccupied. I had a bad feeling about it, though. The couple, Nicole and Nate, ended up renting a room at Mrs. MacDonald's. And early this morning, Nicole rings her friends to tell them that Nate has disappeared without a trace. Sound familiar?"

Inspector Reid stared at Dessie for a moment before his gaze drifted toward the reception area. "Rosa said you came with a group of young people. I assume one of them is Nicole?"

"Yes," Dessie confirmed. "The other two are Val and Sam, the couple that stayed with me. I drove us here."

Inspector Reid stood up and ran a hand through his hair. "Thank you, Mrs. McKendrick. I'd like to talk to Nicole now."

"Let me give you some more information for the report so you don't have to look it up in the system," Dessie said, pointing her chin toward the computer. "I'd be happy to come in any time to sign the statement."

Inspector Reid sighed and scratched his cheek.

"That won't be necessary, Mrs. McKendrick. Let me talk to Nicole, then we'll contact friends and relatives, and I'm sure, as in ninety percent of all cases, this will resolve itself." When Dessie tried to object, he cut her off. "Let's not get ahead of ourselves just yet. He was there when Nicole went to bed last night, and it is," he looked at his wristwatch again, "only eight o'clock. I know this is a sensitive subject for you, with your history, but the likelihood that this Nate..."

"Inspector Reid." Dessie spoke through clenched teeth. His condescending tone annoyed her beyond measure, but she knew there was no use getting emotional if she wanted to be taken seriously by the inspector. "I insist that you at least write a report with my statement. I know how these things go. I remember it all too well. Everything needs to be done by the book this time, so I can't be fobbed off when I follow up on this."

Inspector Reid looked at her for a moment and then sat down, clearly resigned. He shifted a few documents back and forth on his desk and found a blank sheet of paper in the chaos. "Well then, full name?"

"Desdemona LaFleur."

DI Reid, pen already on paper, paused and looked at her in disbelief.

"McKendrick is my husband's name. When we got married, he took my name. LaFleur. So that's the name that's on my passport. Desdemona LaFleur. Since my husband's disappearance, I've gone by McKendrick."

Dessie held Inspector Reid's gaze defiantly. She could guess what was going on in his head. He didn't exactly have a poker face. Finally, he wrote down the name, asked her a few more questions about herself, and asked for her phone number.

"So, Mrs. LaFleur...uh...McKendrick, I'd really like to talk to Nicole next. It's very kind of you to bring her and her friends here, but I can arrange for them to get back to Tarbet. There is no need for you to wait around at the station. I'm sure you are a busy lady, running your B&B and all." When Dessie was about to disagree, he quickly continued. "Look, I understand you think there's a connection between this event and your husband's disappearance. It seems to be more than just a coincidence. I assure you, if that is indeed the case, I will take the investigation seriously. But I need to check facts with Nicole first."

Dessie couldn't keep her feelings to herself any longer. "I know that, Inspector. But you have to believe me, there's something wrong. My gut tells me—"

time cleaner with an agency in Helensburgh. She sent Andie a check every month, but the small amount wasn't even enough to pay the rent. Andie, feeling guilty enough for taking her parents' money but knowing they wanted to contribute to her education, never complained.

With a heavy heart, Andie had declined the Crump and Kendall offer. At least they had given her the prospect of a semester internship, so she had hopefully not completely wasted this great opportunity.

However, she didn't want to get into her financial difficulties with Sarah. And she definitely wouldn't explain how a vision had derailed her plans completely.

"Unfortunately, that didn't work out," she said, trying to sound cheerful. "And I found a good job here, so I came home for the summer."

"Really?" Sarah sounded skeptical. "To Tarbet? Aren't you bored out of your mind?"

"It's true that there isn't much going on here." Andie tried to keep her voice cheerful. "But hey, at least, I am not spending any money and can save up a bunch. Enjoy the movie. I hope I can still see it when I get back to Edinburgh. The closest cinema here is over twenty-five miles away."

"You poor thing," Sarah said. "Couldn't you have found a job in Edinburgh? One that pays better?"

"Maybe, but...there's another reason I'm spending the summer here. It's...a family thing." It wasn't that far from the truth.

Sarah seemed satisfied with that explanation and soon said goodbye.

CHAPTER SIX

DESSIE

Dessie was in no hurry to get back to Tarbet. She would rather have stayed at the police station, waiting to see what would come out of Nicole's interview. But there was no point in stubbornly resisting the inspector's wishes. That would have helped no one.

She had to admit to herself that she might have been a little too aggressive. She could have given Inspector Reid the benefit of the doubt. Her experience with his predecessor, Inspector Murray, who had always rolled his eyes at her concerns and theories, had probably made her a little prejudiced.

But she didn't know what else she could do to make the police listen! A familiar feeling of helplessness and despair washed over her, and Dessie felt tears welling up in her eyes.

Of course the inspector had to verify her story and speak to Nicole before taking any action. Ashamed and angry at herself, Dessie wiped the tears from her cheeks as she recalled how she had stormed into the police station like a madwoman and how she had basically charged at Inspector Reid.

quickly jumped to her mark and focused on her performance as the curtain opened.

That afternoon, everything went like clockwork. Their timing was perfect, and nobody forgot their lines. The five people in the audience all laughed in the right places. Afterward, three audience members even gave them a standing ovation, including the man with the flowers. Dessie was pretty sure that his attention was on her. Amy was on the other side of the stage. If the admirer wasn't completely cross-eyed, it really was Dessie he was clapping for.

Her adrenaline high after their most successful performance to date, Dessie gave in to one of her fits of spontaneity, as Amy called them. Her face still painted with the blue and red alien make-up, she jumped to the auditorium side of the room after the last curtain call.

The young man was in the process of handing the flowers to Tom when he noticed Dessie's arrival. She took a deep breath and smiled at him.

"Hi," she said. Luckily, he couldn't see her bright red face under the theater paint.

"Hi." The stranger returned a dazzling smile.

"Umm, I wanted to thank you for the flowers."

The man didn't reply, just looked at her with his intense blue eyes.

Okay, this was awkward. She abruptly regretted being so forward. "At least, I thought they were for me…did I get that wrong? Were they for—"

"Yes, they were definitely for you. Definitely." He had a slight American accent, which made him seem even more like a movie star. Suddenly, it occurred to her that he might even be a celebrity, with the film festival in town and all. Someone who looked like that had to be famous… She got completely flustered, and her skin began to itch under all the make-up.

He held out his hand. "Connor. Connor McKendrick."

"Dessie," she replied in a hoarse voice.

~

DESSIE CRANED HER NECK, but she couldn't see Connor anywhere in the crowded pub. She had been lucky to get a small table in the back, but now she feared Conner wouldn't be able to see her. Maybe she should have waited for him at the bar, but she didn't want to risk losing these seats. For the dozenth time, she looked at her watch and took a small sip of cider. He wasn't late. She had just arrived way too early.

Finally, she saw him making his way through the cheerful crowd. The fleeting thought crossed her mind that these people were celebrating positive reviews and sell-out shows, but before envy could take hold of her, Conner's brilliant smile fully captured her attention. What did it matter if the first Edinburgh Festival she performed at wasn't her big break? Of course, she had dreamed of it. But she knew that the road to a successful acting career was a long and rocky one. Amy always told her not to be so serious and just enjoy the experience.

Connor waved, pointing to the bar and then to her glass, raising his eyebrows questioningly. She shook her head and smiled. She still had plenty to drink. Somehow, Connor got the bartender's attention right away, unlike Dessie, who had waited her turn for a good ten minutes earlier. Connor soon came to her table with a pint of beer.

"Hi," he greeted her. "I'm sorry it's so busy here. If I would have known, I would have suggested a quieter place. Somewhere where we can talk properly."

"I don't mind," Dessie assured him. She braced herself for an awkward silence, which usually happened on a first date, until they either found a common topic or drank so much that the topic no longer mattered. But there was no awkwardness at all. Connor just calmly took a sip of beer, leaned back, and looked at her. "Desdemona LaFleur," he said slowly, emphasizing each syllable. The way he said it, it sounded like a poem. "When I read your name in the festival program, I knew I had to see you in that play. I hope it's not a stage name!"

Dessie blushed. "Most people think I made it up, but no, that's really my name." Before self-consciousness could take over, she said on impulse, "But who knows, maybe the name has something to do with why I've dreamed of being on stage ever since I was little." She rarely revealed such things about herself, at least not on a first date, but there was something about Connor that made her open up to him.

Only two hours later, it seemed completely natural to Dessie that Connor sat next to her on the wooden bench with his arm around her. Their empty glasses stood forgotten on the table, and Dessie had tuned out the noisy pub crowd. They might as well have been on a desert island.

"So how do you like Canterbury?" Connor asked. She had told him she was doing an undergraduate degree in drama at the University of Kent. "I've never been to the Southeast."

"And I've never really left Kent," Dessie sighed. "Until now, that is. My father lives in Ashford, but he didn't move there until I went to boarding school in Maidstone. Before that we lived in Whitstable, which is on the coast, near Canterbury. So, umm, I don't really think of Ashford as my home. And Canterbury, well, it's a great city, a great campus...a perfect little student town. I don't really see myself staying there after I graduate, though." She shrugged.

"You said your father lives in Ashford?" Connor asked. "Are your parents divorced?"

Dessie looked down at her hands in her lap. "My mother died when I was fourteen. A stroke. It was very sudden." She looked up, saw the sadness in Connor's blue eyes, and managed to come up with a small smile. "After her death, my father sent me to boarding school. We never had a great relationship, and it was just weird without Mom. She, well, she had kind of been the link between us, the one who held the family together. Without her..." Dessie lowered her gaze again.

Before Connor could say anything, Dessie laughed nervously. "You should be a therapist. I hardly know you, but now I've already told you my entire life story. I'm sorry. You must be tired of hearing about me." Dessie realized she had learned nothing about Connor yet. Maybe he *was* a therapist. Although she still secretly hoped she'd been right about her movie-star theory. "Tell me about yourself. What do you do for a living?"

"Oh, that's boring," Connor brushed her off. "I work in the financial sector as an advisor for private investors. I find your life much more interesting. I'd like to know all there is to know about you. So you don't have any siblings?"

No one had ever paid as much attention to Dessie as Connor did. She felt flattered. More than that, she felt understood. Perhaps for the first time in her life.

Dessie leaned against Connor and gazed up at him. She felt safe with him, as if she had finally arrived at a long-awaited destination.

≈

"Hɪ, Aᴍʏ," Dessie shouted excitedly into her cell phone. "Guess where I am?"

"Hey," Amy replied sleepily. "You're in Edinburgh. Aren't you?" Amy seemed to be using the term break to catch up on the sleep she had missed in Canterbury. It was almost noon, but it appeared that Dessie had woken her friend with the phone call.

"No, I'm in Gretna Green."

"Okaaayyy," Amy drew out the last syllable. Dessie waited anxiously, but her friend's brain wasn't fully functioning yet. "And what are you doing there?" Amy yawned.

"Well, what does one do in Gretna Green?" Dessie became impatient. "I got married!"

"What?" Amy suddenly seemed wide awake.

"Yes, Connor and I got married."

Her announcement was answered with silence. Dessie had expected a very different reaction, and disappointment washed over her.

"But..." Finally, Amy found words to express what she was feeling. "You guys barely know each other."

"We've known each other for a year!"

"Holy hell, Dessie! Have you gone nuts? You don't just marry the guy. You've seen each other three times during that year, just a few weeks at a time. He hasn't even come to see you in Canterbury. You always went to Edinburgh, spending all your money…"

"That's right. Our current situation meant we could hardly see each other." Dessie was upset that she had to defend her actions to Amy. "We want to be together properly. We love each other too much for a long-distance relationship."

"Well then, do things in the proper order. Move in together…" Amy seemed to struggle with her words, as if she found Dessie so unreasonable that she couldn't find a way to get through to her. Dessie didn't even recognize her bubbly friend. Usually, Amy was the carefree one, persuading Dessie to have more fun.

Now it seemed as if Amy couldn't even be happy for her. What kind of friend reacted that way to such wonderful news? Dessie got a little worked up as Amy continued. "How are you planning on making this work? I assume he's moving to Canterbury? He hasn't even been here once."

"No, I'm moving to Edinburgh." Dessie knew she sounded petulant, but she didn't care. This was her wedding day, and her so-called best friend was ruining it for her.

"Dessie!" Amy sounded genuinely distressed. "You can't drop out of university for him. Don't do that."

"Oh, I don't know what I'm doing yet. Maybe I'll transfer to the University of Edinburgh. Or I'll just get a part-time job. It might not even be necessary. Connor makes a good living."

"And what about our plans? Moving to London after graduation? Going to auditions together?"

Dessie's anger dissipated somewhat when she realized Amy was probably jealous of her happiness. Jealous, and probably sad that her best friend was going away. She hadn't thought of that and felt a little guilty.

"I'm sorry, Amy." Dessie's voice was much softer now. "Yes, we had made those plans. But that was before I met the love of my life. When you meet your Prince Charming, you'll understand. You are so sociable, and everyone likes you. You won't have any trouble making new friends in London..."

"That's not my point at all." Now Amy sounded annoyed. "At least, it's not just about that. Do you really want to give up your dreams for this man? A man you don't even really know?"

Tears sprung to Dessie's eyes. Why was her friend giving her such a hard time? Why couldn't she just be happy for her? There was nobody else in her life she could share her joy with. Her father would, as usual, muster up little interest in this important change in his daughter's life. If he got upset about it, she could count herself lucky.

"Thanks a lot, Amy!" Dessie blurted out bitterly. "I probably shouldn't be surprised you're trying to ruin this for me. You were against my relationship with Connor from the beginning."

"That's not true at all!" Amy sounded genuinely surprised. "I told you I thought he was nice. The one time I met him. He didn't seem interested in getting to know me. He was charming, I'll give him that. I just…thought he gave little about himself away. You know next to nothing about him. And then I didn't like that you were the one making all the effort. Traveling to him every time…I don't know. I thought it was strange after he had gone through so much trouble getting to know you. With the flowers and everything."

Amy *was* jealous, Dessie was sure now. And envious that she, the less attractive of the two of them, had found such a fairy-tale prince.

What she said wasn't even true. Connor was, in fact, very attentive to her. He took her out to dinner and gave her presents all the time.

Earlier, just after they'd left the picturesque old Blacksmiths Shop where they had been married, Connor had fetched her a package from the car.

"A wedding present," he'd told her.

Dessie couldn't believe it. "When did you buy that? We've been together the entire time. When did you have time to go to a store?"

"Open it and you'll see."

Dessie had sat down on a bench in the small park behind the Blacksmiths Shop. The gift was quite heavy. She tore open the paper with great anticipation. Inside was an antique tin music box. Connor showed her how to wind it up. Animals and wagons of a traveling circus moved around in a circle to circus music.

"The music box belonged to my mother," Connor said. "And before that, my grandmother. It's old, an heirloom. It just felt right to give it to you. And maybe we can pass it on to our daughter one day."

Dessie hadn't been able to hold back the tears as she threw her arms around her new husband. He hadn't really talked about his family, but Dessie was under the impression that both his parents had passed away. He wasn't the type to dwell on the past. "Everyone is the author of their own future," he said frequently. "It starts with focusing on the present, not on what you can't change anymore, the past."

Dessie admired him. After all, she knew how hard it was to get over the loss of a loved one. That was one thing they had in common.

As far as Dessie had been concerned, this gesture, this gift, was worth much more than a thousand words. It showed her how much she meant to him and that she was now his family.

But she couldn't explain all that to Amy now. She didn't want to defend their love, anyway. All she wanted was to share her happiness with her best friend. Connor was patiently waiting in the expensive restaurant he had chosen to celebrate their nuptials because he knew this phone call was important to her.

And now she had to deal with Amy's antagonistic reaction, Dessie thought bitterly. She wasn't even really listening anymore when her friend asked, "What about your dreams, Dessie? The acting career? Are you going to give it all up? For him?"

She had kept Connor waiting long enough, Dessie decided. Dreams could change. She had unexpectedly met the man of her dreams. With Connor, she had found a home. A place where she belonged: by his side. Amy didn't seem to understand that.

"Bye, Amy," she said, with a hunch that this might be the last time she talked to her friend. "I have to go now."

DESSIE HADN'T THOUGHT about Amy for a long, long time, and now, as she stared out at the lake, the mountains, and the passing clouds, she wondered what had become of her. For a brief moment, as nostalgia and regret threatened to overwhelm her, she considered tracking Amy down. But she knew she never would. She told herself that it was pride that kept her from doing so, but deep inside she knew it was shame.

She had put aside her dreams, turned her back on friends whose help she could have used then—and now. She had put her life on hold; indeed, you could say she had thrown it away. And there was nothing she could say to Amy that would justify all that. There was only one reason Dessie could give, and Amy wouldn't understand it. At best, she would only pity Dessie.

Dessie had loved Connor more than her life. He had never had anyone but her. And she, since her mother's death at least, had never had anyone but him. She could not, would not, give up on him.

CHAPTER SEVEN

ANDIE

Andie wiped her hands on her apron. When she saw Dessie walk over to the table where Val, Sam, and Nicole were sitting, she listened closely.

"Still no news, Nicole?" her boss asked, as she set down the plates with the guests' breakfast. Nicole, who had moved into Dessie's B&B on the day of Nate's disappearance three days ago, shook her head. Her big eyes looked sadder and sadder every day. Sam seemed to be increasingly worried about his friend, and Val's bad temper got progressively worse.

Dessie kept asking about the investigation, but Nicole didn't seem to mind. "So what does Inspector Reid claim to be doing?"

Nicole just shrugged, but Sam answered for her.

"The police have been contacting Nate's parents, relatives, and friends. When it turned out he hadn't been in touch with anyone, they tracked his phone. It was found in the woods, not far from the Thistle Inn."

Mrs. MacDonald's house was on the outskirts of the village, right on the edge of Argyll Forest Park. The national park was a vast expanse of woodland on the Highland Boundary Fault, the dividing line between the Highlands and Lowlands, with hills and valleys crisscrossed by footpaths.

Andie gnawed on her lower lip, completely forgetting about her task of cutting tomatoes. The find didn't disprove the theory that Nate had gone for a walk. He could have just lost his phone and later injured himself, unable to call for help...

The police had apparently drawn the same conclusion.

"They have sent out search parties to comb the forest," Sam said. "No sign of Nate so far."

Sam gazed at Nicole with concern.

She had tears in her eyes as she pushed the plate with fried eggs and bacon aside, as if talking about the futile search efforts had spoiled her appetite. Andie felt sorry for her. Dessie could have let the poor girl eat before interrogating her.

"We weren't even allowed to join in with the search. On TV, they always ask everyone to help. Community effort and all that. But nobody in Tarbet seems to care that our friend has disappeared," Val grumbled. "I don't know why we're still here. We might as well continue our trip. There is nothing for us to do. Actually, there is nothing to do here at all," she added quietly, rolling her eyes.

"I'm going to stay here until they find Nate...until he's back, I mean..." Nicole broke off, crying. She wiped her face with a napkin.

"We'll stay as well. Obviously, we won't leave you dealing with this by yourself. Val doesn't mean it," Sam comforted her.

Dessie tapped her foot restlessly. "And you've heard nothing from the police regarding Mrs. MacDonald?"

"What do you mean?" Nicole asked.

"Has she been properly questioned?"

"Inspector Reid spoke to her. But she didn't hear Nate leaving or anything." Nicole answered listlessly.

"Yes, but…" Dessie began to object in a loud voice, then apparently changed her mind. Her face changed to its usual guarded expression, and she stepped away from the table. "Enjoy your food."

Andie was used to the fact that Dessie wasn't exactly chatty. But for the rest of the morning, as they continued to serve breakfast, cleaned up, and turned over the rooms, her boss was virtually silent.

Back in the kitchen, shortly before the end of Andie's shift, Dessie cleared her throat and asked, "Would you mind unloading the dishwasher and tidying the kitchen by yourself? I have a call to make and would like to catch them before they leave for their lunch break."

"Yes, of course, no problem."

Andie started taking plates out of the dishwasher and took a stack to the cupboard next to the door. It was ajar, and she could overhear Dessie's agitated voice.

"I just don't understand how you can dismiss the whole thing as a coincidence! Mrs. MacDonald must have something to do with the disappearances!"

Andie guessed her boss was talking to the inspector again. She sounded desperate.

Dessie obviously didn't believe in coincidences.

Neither did Andie. But that had little to do with belief. After all, she knew Mrs. MacDonald's involvement wasn't a coincidence.

AFTER FINISHING work a little later than usual, Andie jumped onto her bike and hurried to Fisherman's Café.

She was aware that Fionna would be uncomfortable waiting there by herself. Fionna had been born and raised in Tarbet, just like Andie, so she knew everyone, too. She could chat with any of the familiar regulars at Fisherman's. But Fionna was antisocial. She preferred a computer screen between herself and another person. Her personality was the complete opposite of her mother's. Rosa was very good with people and actively took part in village life.

When Andie arrived ten minutes later than arranged, she spotted Fionna right away amid the busy lunchtime crowd. Her friend's bright red hair made her stand out.

Fionna waved, and Andie pushed through the people waiting for tables and to-go orders. She slid onto the wooden bench opposite Fionna.

"Sorry, I already ordered. I was starving." Fionna scrunched her freckled nose.

At that moment, Fred, the owner of Fisherman's, put a plate piled high with eggs, bacon, black pudding, mushrooms, tomatoes, sausages, hash browns, and fried bread on the table. Everything was drenched in grease, and Andie shuddered in disgust.

She had nothing against the occasional good Scottish fry-up, but cooking hearty breakfasts had spoiled her appetite a bit. Fred had no competition in Tarbet, and there were always starving hikers during tourist season, so his food wasn't exactly top notch. He put the emphasis on quantity rather than quality.

Fionna didn't seem bothered by that, though. "I haven't had breakfast yet," she said with a full mouth. Fionna was, one could say, self-employed. She lived with her mother and could do as she pleased, so she kept to her own schedule.

Fionna's mother, who worked as a receptionist at the police station in Helensburgh, had long since given up preparing meals for her daughter or encouraging her to cook for herself. Fionna really only left the house for the all-day breakfast at Fisherman's Café. Usually, she just picked up a to-go order. Andie didn't want to imagine what that breakfast looked like after everything was thrown together in a white Styrofoam box.

Well, by the looks of how Fionna shoveled the food into her mouth, she seemed to enjoy it. Andie noticed that her curvy friend had put on even more weight since she had seen her last. Fionna's lifestyle was not doing her any favors. Andie was worried, but she knew Fionna would only react defensively if she expressed her concern.

"I'll have a cup of tea and...a BLT," she placed her order with Fred. When the proprietor left, she leaned forward. "Any news?"

Fionna took a sip of tea and said, "That's what I was going to ask you. You're right at the source, aren't you?"

Fionna might not be one for socializing in person, but she was up on all the gossip. This was mostly because of her mother, who had her fingers in many pies, but it was also because of Fionna's active presence on social media.

"Well, you know Dessie's not much of a talker." Andie nodded her thanks to Fred, who set a mug of tea down in front of her. "But today I heard something. Dessie was talking to DI Reid on the phone, berating him for not arresting Mrs. MacDonald or something like that. She couldn't believe that the criminal mastermind was still at large." Andie couldn't help but sound slightly sarcastic. At the same time, she felt sorry for Dessie, and guilt washed over her. After all, this wasn't a joking matter for her boss. "I don't know how the conversation ended, but if Dessie finally beats the inspector down and he starts to look into—"

"Don't worry," Fionna waved it off. "My mother convinced him Mrs. MacDonald couldn't possibly have anything to do with this. A single frail old lady without male relatives to do the heavy lifting…how on earth might she have incapacitated two strong young men like Connor McKendrick and Nate Saunders? And carried them out of the house into the woods, to hide them where nobody would find them? That would just be ridiculous."

Fionna sounded superior, and Andie, despite her derisive tone earlier, felt annoyed by that. She didn't like the fact that Dessie was being taken for a fool, because her boss didn't deserve that. She felt she had to defend and protect Dessie and was about to say something when she thought better of it.

Besides, she really couldn't blame Fionna for finding the very idea that Mrs. MacDonald could be put behind bars laughable. It was unthinkable and would never happen.

"So Inspector Reid won't bother Mrs. MacDonald?" she asked Fionna instead. The young woman popped the last piece of sausage into her mouth and pushed the empty plate away from her, shaking her head vigorously. "No. Right now, the working theory is that Nate went into the woods voluntarily, maybe to go for a morning walk. They found his phone, but nothing else, and they assume he must have dropped it accidentally. He might have gotten lost in the woods or injured himself."

"Yes, I heard about the search parties," Andie said. "Do you think this could be a problem for us? Maybe they'll find…"

"It's already been taken care of. They won't find anything," Fionna interrupted her.

Andie nodded. "I was half expecting the meeting to be canceled. We don't want to be interrupted by park rangers."

"The searchers go home as soon as it gets dark."

Andie gave another nod. "That means we're definitely

meeting tonight, then." She didn't have to ask her friend whether she would come. Antisocial or not, this was a different matter. Fionna had no trouble venturing out after dark to be in the company of her sisters.

"Of course. It's important that we do it tonight. It can't be put off."

CHAPTER EIGHT

DESSIE

Dessie tried to ignore the itch. The Highlands were teeming with midges in the summer. There seemed to be an entire army of them here, at the edge of the forest behind the Thistle Inn.

It annoyed her she hadn't prepared better and used that lotion the locals swore was a secret weapon against the little beasts. But then, the decision to go to Mrs. MacDonald's house had been rather spontaneous.

Grayson, whose trip to Paris had been canceled and who'd kept her company every evening since Nate's disappearance, had said his goodbye for the night. Contrary to habit, Dessie had poured herself another glass of wine as she paced the kitchen. Apparently, talking poor Grayson's ear off about her frustration with the police had done nothing to calm her down. Talking didn't seem to be a solution. She had to do something. Without thinking it through, she'd thrown on a jacket and gone for a walk, finally finding herself lurking behind Mrs. MacDonald's house.

A flood of memories from her stay with Connor ten years ago assaulted her, and it was almost as bad as the midges. From where she was standing, she had a clear view of the guest room window. She could even make out the rectangle of paper stuck to the glass pane. It was a hand-written warning not to leave the window open to keep the midges out. The note had been yellow with age back then, and it was still stuck there.

Dessie had to assume that the old-fashioned furnishings hadn't changed either. She wondered if Nate and Nicole had slept in that room, too, or in the other guest room with the window facing the street. Her gut told her they had shared the same room as Connor and her, but by this point, she didn't know if she could trust her gut anymore.

Unsure of what to do, Dessie left the cover of the trees and stepped over the fence. The grass on Mrs. MacDon-ald's back lawn was tall, almost up to her knees. She edged toward the dark window. She couldn't really make out anything in the shadows of the dark room. The window next to it was the bathroom, she remembered, and it was dark, too.

Dessie moved along the back of the house until she reached the corner and cautiously peered around it. The next house was a little ways off, on the other side of the path that led into the woods. There was nobody on the road in front of the Thistle Inn, so she dared to venture on.

The next window was lit up. Heart pounding, she crept up to it, took a deep breath, and glanced in. Lace curtains hid the lower half, but if she stood on her tiptoes, she could see a slice of what appeared to be Mrs. MacDonald's living room. The TV and a lamp on the side table were on, but the big armchair facing the television was empty. She craned her neck but was reasonably sure that Mrs. MacDonald wasn't in the room at all.

At that moment, she heard a bang. The front door! Dessie quickly retreated behind the house, ducking behind the tall grass.

The old lady must have heard her and was now investigating the noise. Panicked, Dessie looked around. Did she dare move across the lawn, climb the fence, and hide behind the trees? Or should she stay, hoping the grass offered enough cover? What if Mrs. MacDonald discovered her in her back garden? Dessie racked her brains for an excuse that explained her presence here so late in the evening.

Before she could decide, Dessie spotted Mrs. MacDonald on the path leading to the woods. Dessie ducked, pressing herself close to the ground. She was wearing dark clothes and hoped she'd blend into the shadows. It was dark, but the moon was full and provided ample light.

Dessie didn't need to worry. Mrs. MacDonald took no notice of her. The old lady wore some kind of loose-fitting cloak and was busy putting the large hood over her head as she walked past Dessie into the woods. She used her walking stick, but Dessie could have sworn the woman was much less stooped and frail-looking than usual. Never mind that, why on earth was the old lady taking a nighttime walk in the woods?

Dessie sprang into action. She had merely followed a hunch by coming here and had been feeling rather silly, but now she realized what her mission was. She had to follow Mrs. MacDonald.

Dessie climbed over the low fence and stepped onto the path. She could barely make out the small figure ahead of her, but she didn't dare close the distance. She didn't want Mrs. MacDonald to hear her. Scared she would lose sight of her, Dessie kept her gaze fixed on the old lady's back. Should Mrs. MacDonald turn around, Dessie was prepared to jump behind the trees lining the path. Every time a twig cracked under her feet or stones rolled noisily away, Dessie stopped and held her breath in panic.

After a while, she calmed down, realizing that she didn't need to be that careful. The old lady seemed to be in a hurry and was walking purposefully. It surprised Dessie that Mrs. MacDonald was in good enough shape to keep that pace. She appeared to have lost all sense of frailty.

Dessie became less afraid of losing sight of her, as she seemed to be sticking to the path that led to Cruach Tairbeirt, the only mountain in this part of the Argyll Forest Park. Actually, it was more a hill, not very impressive compared to the Arrochar Alps, but it still afforded a delightful view. Less than an hour's walk from Tarbet, it was a popular destination for tourists who preferred a leisurely walk rather than a strenuous hike.

But this path seemed to just meander along, and Dessie, who had lost all sense of time, was starting to doubt they would ever get to a destination at all. What on earth was the woman doing, wandering around the woods in the middle of the night?

After coming around a bend, Dessie realized that she had lost sight of Mrs. MacDonald. She suppressed a frustrated groan. Had she been following her for that long, just to lose her?

What was she even doing? She had no business spying on people—and was clearly terrible at it. Well, she would have let the police handle it if that blasted Inspector Reid would take her seriously.

Dessie was about to speed up, hoping to catch up with Mrs. MacDonald, when she noticed a flash in the woods to her left. It was the moonlight bouncing off the old lady's metallic walking stick.

At least that was what Dessie assumed, because she caught a glimpse of a dark figure in a cloak before it disappeared between the trees. Dessie plowed through the thick undergrowth, not even stopping to wonder what the woman was doing, tramping through the woods. How had she managed it, given the uneven ground, thick and thorny bushes, and low-hanging branches? Dessie herself had a difficult time, noisily crashing through the wilderness. She could only hope Mrs. MacDonald was making plenty of noise of her own and wouldn't hear Dessie.

Every once in a while, Dessie stopped to get her heavy breathing under control and try to get her bearings. The bright moon didn't quite penetrate the dense treetops, and she couldn't make out any movement. She had to rely on her hearing to determine which direction to go.

Now the forest seemed dead quiet. No owl or other creature of the night made a sound. There was no rustling or crackling.

Dessie held her breath, but there was no sight or sound of Mrs. MacDonald anywhere. To make matters worse, Dessie had totally lost her sense of direction.

Panic spread through her, and she looked around frantically. All she could make out were the dark outlines of ferns, bushes, and tree trunks. She squinted, staring hard as the trees seemed to blur into the shapes of people standing stock-still, watching her.

A shiver ran down her spine, and she told herself not to let her imagination run wild. She took a deep breath and inhaled the musty smell of wet, decaying leaves and pine needles. At least there weren't any animals close by—that was a good thing in her current situation. Unless... She wouldn't hear silent nighttime hunters, would she? Her mind began to spin with the thought of the animals that could be lurking in the shadows.

Now the forest seemed to awaken, and suddenly she could hear noises everywhere. Scared, Dessie spun around, staring in this direction, then that.

Pull yourself together, she told herself. Taking another few deep breaths, she decided on a direction at random— she had to arrive somewhere at some point, didn't she?—

and kept walking. As she was no longer trying to follow anyone, she could pay more attention to her footing. The last thing she needed was to twist her ankle and get stuck in the middle of nowhere. Her thoughts strayed to Nate. Had that happened to him? The police seemed to think that he had gotten lost and injured himself—

Dessie stopped in her tracks when she caught sight of a bright flicker behind the trees. A fire? Even though she felt fear creep in, Dessie moved toward the light, as it was her only point of reference.

She kept an eye out for Mrs. MacDonald but couldn't detect another soul. Soon she heard a crackling sound and smelled burning wood.

The fire had to be directly in front of her, behind a dense group of pines. Dessie pushed her way through a gap and slowly moved a bunch of ferns that were obstructing her view.

She suppressed a gasp. A person in a dark cape stood not two feet away from her. Dessie's hands trembled, yet she dared not let go of the ferns.

The figure turned slightly, and Dessie saw her profile. Mrs. MacDonald. The old woman took a few steps away from Dessie, and two other cloaked figures appeared next to her. Dessie recognized one of them right away. It was a curvy young woman with red hair she had seen in the village numerous times.

The third woman turned, and the fire illuminated her face. Dessie stifled a scream. It was Rosa, the receptionist at the Helensburgh police station.

Mrs. MacDonald muttered something to Rosa that Dessie couldn't understand. Rosa adjusted the hood of her cloak.

Dessie's eyes fell on the large brooch that fastened the cloak. The shape of a pentacle shone golden in the fire's glow. In the center sparkled a purple gemstone—an amethyst? Dessie squinted until she recognized the gem was the flower of a thistle—the symbol of the Scottish Highlands. Dessie saw that the red-haired young woman and Mrs. MacDonald also wore such a brooch.

Her arm ached from holding the ferns back, but she didn't dare move for fear of being detected by the three women.

Just then, the women stepped further to the side. Her view opened up, and Dessie forgot about the pain in her arm.

At least a dozen cloaked figures formed a circle. Dessie couldn't make out any other faces.

Next to the fire stood a boulder. Black liquid was spilling down its side. There was something on top of the large stone. Dessie strained her eyes to see what it was.

It seemed furry, light gray… Was it a sheep?

As the flames flared up, she suddenly understood what the dark liquid was. It wasn't black at all, it just looked like it in the dark.

It was red.

Blood.

The cloaked figures joined hands and started chanting something in Gaelic.

Dessie didn't speak the ancient language, so she couldn't understand what the women were saying.

She was so spellbound by the sight of what appeared to be a pagan ritual that she didn't pay attention to what was happening around her.

She didn't notice someone creeping up behind her—until she felt a hand on her shoulder. Dessie jumped, letting go of the ferns. She bit her lip, trying not to cry out.

Slowly, very slowly, she turned around. Her heart was beating loudly in her chest, and her throat was so tight that she could hardly breathe.

The hand belonged to a small person swathed in a dark

cloak. The hood was pulled far over her face, so Dessie couldn't make out any features. Straight dark hair spilled around the sides of the hood. Dessie recognized the brooch she had seen on the other figures around the fire.

It took Dessie only a split second to take all this in before her fear took over and she bolted. She rushed around the cloaked figure, clearly taking her by surprise, and charged blindly ahead.

With more luck than good sense, she managed to not run directly into a tree but found a way through the dense undergrowth. Branches, needles, and leaves hit her in the face. But Dessie didn't dare slow down, sure she was being followed.

She dashed through the woods until her foot caught on a branch or a root. Her hand got tangled in bushes as she tried to catch herself, and she fell face first to the ground.

Dessie was so shocked that the pain barely registered as she struggled to turn to her back. She managed to sit up, but when she put weight on her foot to stand, pain shot through her leg.

She couldn't get up. Panicking, she crawled into some dense shrubbery, hoping to hide there from her pursuer.

She tried to determine whether anyone was chasing her, but she couldn't hear anything over her frantic heartbeat and the blood rushing in her ears.

Dessie cowered there for what felt like ages, trying to calm down. It was then that she noticed that her face hurt. She carefully touched her nose, and her fingers came away wet and sticky. She was bleeding. At least her nose didn't appear to be broken.

Sighing, she pricked her ears to listen again.

Silence.

Nobody was following her.

Dessie slid along the damp ground until she could reach a tree trunk to pull herself upright. As soon as she put pressure on her foot, pain coursed through her. She tried to move along on one foot, jumping and holding on to tree trunks and branches, but it soon proved impossible on the uneven, overgrown ground.

She dropped to her hands and knees, crawling along.

Dessie tried not to cry and desperately attempted to stifle the feeling of doom that threatened to take hold of her. She didn't know where she was or how to get out of the forest. How long would she have to crawl around before she found someone to help her? How long would she have the strength to go on? And what if she wasn't going anywhere at all, but moving around in circles?

Dessie struggled up a small embankment toward a sliver of moonlight. Tears of relief sprang to her eyes as she found herself on a footpath. She could only hope that it was the one she and Mrs. MacDonald had been on. But which way to Tarbet? She didn't want to head farther into the forest.

She should pick a direction, but she didn't want to take the chance of being wrong. Her knees hurt, her hands were cut up and bleeding, the pain in her ankle seemed unbearable, and her nose was throbbing and numb.

Exhausted, Dessie stretched out flat on her back on the path. For a while she just lay there, listening to her own breathing, feeling the cold of the ground penetrating her clothes, her flesh, her bones.

There was no way around it.

She would have to call for help.

She would be lucky if she had cell reception—and if anyone could even find her.

With what felt like the last of her strength, she pulled her phone out of her pocket and tapped the name of the only person she could call.

"Grayson," she said as he picked up. "I need you!"

CHAPTER NINE

ANDIE

W hen Andie arrived at Dessie's B&B the next morning, Grayson greeted her in the hallway.

"Can you stay all day today and take over Dessie's chores? I can help with breakfast if it's too much for one person. Dessie had an accident. It's been a long night, and I don't want to wake her. She should rest."

"Of course I can cover for her," Andie replied. "An accident? What happened? Is she okay?" She walked past Grayson so he couldn't see her face.

"She sprained her ankle, and she has some cuts and bruises," Grayson explained as he followed her into the kitchen.

Andie immediately busied herself with setting the tables. "How did that happen?" She tried to keep her tone casual.

"She went for a walk in the woods last night and took a tumble."

Andie chewed her lower lip. She really needed to talk to Dessie herself, as soon as she was awake.

"I drove her to the hospital, and we only got back a few hours ago. As you can imagine, Dessie was completely exhausted. You know what she's like. I had to convince her she should take some time to recover today. I reassured her we would take care of everything." Grayson gave Andie his signature dazzling smile.

Andie had paid little attention to that smile before, but now she noticed that something bothered her about it. Maybe it was because of the unnaturally white teeth…it seemed a bit…fake.

"Dessie can count on you, can't she, Andie?"

There was something threatening in his voice, even though his expression seemed so friendly.

"Of course she can," Andie muttered, wondering what Dessie had told Grayson about last night.

Andie kept herself occupied preparing breakfast for the guests. She avoided looking at Grayson as best as she could.

Luckily, it was busy. Almost all the guests came in at the same time. Grayson took orders and served the food and drinks Andie prepared.

Nicole came in by herself and stared at her cup of coffee and her fried egg before leaving again.

When the rush was over, Val and Sam had yet to arrive. Andy silently prayed for them to come for breakfast already, as she didn't want to stand idly in the kitchen with Grayson. What if he asked her questions about last night?

For the first time, she was glad to hear Val's penetrating voice as the two remaining guests entered the breakfast room.

"I'm tired of sitting around here. I want to get out of this miserable, boring village."

"Shh," Sam seemed embarrassed for his rude girlfriend and looked at Andie with a contrite smile.

Andie led them to a table before Grayson could beat her to it. "Good morning!"

"That's debatable," Sam grumbled. Andie was a little

taken aback. She had never known him to be anything but friendly and solicitous.

"What can I get you today? The usual?" she blurted, trying to gloss over the tense atmosphere. Sam and Val just nodded.

Andie went to the kitchen to prepare breakfast for the couple, glad that Grayson didn't know what their usual was. He had no choice but to step aside and find something else to do.

After a few minutes of uncomfortable silence, Val hissed, "Give me one good reason for sticking around."

"Our friend is missing," Sam replied in a tone that implied that wasn't the first time he's said it today. He clearly was fed up with stating the obvious. "Something bad might have happened to him. Don't you care about him at all? How can you be so coldhearted?"

"They won't find him any sooner if we mope around here, twiddling our thumbs. It will not help him if I waste my summer break. I'm not coldhearted. I'm just not a hypocrite like you."

Sam's eyes widened.

Andie brought the plates with fried eggs and bacon to their table, retreating quickly.

"What do you mean, hypocrite?" Sam waited to ask until Andie was back in the kitchen, even though she could still hear him.

"Nate's not your friend. We hardly know him. He only came along as Nicole's boyfriend."

"Yes, he is Nicole's boyfriend. And she's our friend. She's devastated, and she needs us."

Andie scrubbed the large pan, creating some noise. The running water didn't drown out Val's voice, though, when she slapped her hands on the table and cried, "See! I knew it. All you care about is Nicole."

"Of course I care about her. She's a friend, and something terrible happened to her—"

"I'll bet you're secretly glad that Nate is gone, so you
have every excuse to comfort Nicole." Val had probably
intended to mock him, but the note of bitterness in her
voice was unmistakable.

"Oh, come on!" Now Sam raised his voice, too.

Andie put the pan on the draining rack and wiped her
hands on her apron, trying not to look directly at the
arguing couple. She noticed Grayson casually leaning
against the refrigerator, unabashedly watching the two
young people. They didn't seem to notice, though.

"Just admit it," Val shouted. "You're not really hoping
Nate will return alive and well. Then you can have Nicole
to yourself."

All eyes went to the door, which had just slammed shut
with a bang. Nicole stood in the breakfast room, looking
thunderstruck.

Her lips trembled. Sam was out of his chair in a flash,
putting his arms around Nicole's narrow shoulders. "Please
don't cry. She doesn't mean it," he said softly.

With a loud clatter, Val threw her fork onto her plate of
uneaten breakfast, jumped up, and rushed past Sam and
Nicole.

"Come on, let's take a walk," Sam said, his arm still
around Nicole. "We'll get some fresh air."

Andie quickly cleared the table, threw the eggs and
bacon in the garbage, and put the last of the plates and
cutlery in the dishwasher. Why was Grayson still standing
in the kitchen? There was nothing for him to do. She was
just about to say, "I've got this," when she heard the
kitchen door again.

This time, it was Dessie. Andie smiled at her
uncertainly.

Dessie just nodded, hobbling into the room on crutches. Her hair was a mess, and she had dark circles under her eyes. Her outfit was more casual than usual: sweatpants, thick wool socks, an oversize T-shirt, and a gray cardigan. She eyed them both. "What's going on here?"

"You're supposed to be sleeping." Grayson hurried to lead Dessie to a table and helped her sit down.

"The guests are too noisy. Besides, I've slept enough. I don't want to lie in bed all day."

Grayson pulled up a chair and placed Dessie's foot on it, cupping his hand underneath. "I bet this hard chair isn't comfortable. Should I get a cushion?"

"Oh, it's fine," Dessie waved her hand. It didn't escape Andie's notice, however, that she looked secretly pleased that Grayson made a fuss.

"No, I insist," Grayson said, frowning as he looked around. "Do we have any seat cushions?"

"Well, there are some on the bench under the coat rack in the hallway," Dessie suggested hesitantly. Grayson nodded. "Andie, will you get one, please?"

Get it yourself, Andie thought, eager to be alone with Dessie. Instead, she just said, "Of course," through clenched teeth and moved into the hallway.

When Andie returned with the seat cushion, Grayson had pulled up a chair to the table beside Dessie's. He was still holding her bandaged foot in his hand, and he was leaning so close to her boss that Andie almost felt like she was intruding. She cleared her throat and walked over to hand Grayson the cushion.

Ordinarily, she and Dessie would make the beds and change the sheets now. Would Grayson help with that, too? She didn't want to ask and just stood there indecisively.

"Be a good girl and make us some coffee, would you?" Grayson didn't even look at Andie when he asked, but kept his attention on Dessie. "I'm sure you could use some caffeine."

Andie tried not to show her annoyance.

She really wanted to speak to Dessie alone, but Grayson made no move to leave her side. As Andie made the coffee, the two of them stuck their heads together and whispered. Dessie even giggled at something the American said. Andie sure hoped her boss's unusual behavior had something to do with the painkillers she was taking.

Once she had put two mugs of coffee on the table, she went back to the kitchen, scrubbing at nonexistent stains on the countertop.

Finally, Dessie raised her voice. "Andie, would you vacuum the guest rooms and the corridor and make the beds, please? Oh, and the shared bathroom and the room four en suite need cleaning, too." Her boss blushed, as usual uncomfortable with giving orders.

"Sure, no problem." Andie really wanted to know what Grayson and Dessie were talking about, so she pretended to close the door behind her and stood there, listening intently.

"Do you have your phone on you?" she heard Dessie say. "Can I borrow it?"

"Here you go."

"This is Dessie McKendrick. I would like to speak to Inspector Reid."

At that moment, the door to room number two opened. Andie hurried down the hallway before she was caught eavesdropping.

Begrudgingly, she set about her task of stripping the beds in the vacant rooms. She really would have liked to know what Dessie had to say to the inspector. She was not worried about the police investigation, but it would have been useful to hear Dessie's account of what had happened last night.

Her thoughts drifted to Grayson. She wondered what bothered her about him. She had paid little attention to him so far, as she hadn't been aware of his close friendship with Dessie. He hadn't been on Andie's radar, so to speak, but now she decided to find out more about him.

Making the beds took longer than usual because she had to complete the task by herself, but Andie also took her time cleaning. She kept trying to talk to Dessie in private, but every time she found a pretext to see her, Grayson was with her.

When she was finally finished with all her tasks, she went back to the kitchen, surprised to find Grayson cooking a meal for Dessie. He looked as if he was right at home in the B&B.

"I can stay and check in guests if you need me to," Andie said to Dessie.

"Oh no, thanks, Grayson offered to do that."

Andie eyed Grayson suspiciously. "Okay, is there anything else…"

"No, that's all right. You can go home. But if you don't mind," Dessie smiled sheepishly, "can you work extra hours for the next couple of days, too? I'm afraid I'm going to be laid up with this stupid injury for a bit longer."

"No problem. I'm here if you need me," Andie said, still looking at Grayson, hoping it would trigger a vision, or at least an intuitive feeling about him.

She only noticed that she had been staring at him for too long when Dessie cleared her throat.

Andie blushed. "Okay, bye, see you tomorrow. Hope you feel better."

She was so annoyed with herself that she left her jacket hanging in the hallway as she left the B&B.

To make matters worse, she ran into Inspector Reid right outside the door. Andie would really have liked to eavesdrop on Dessie's conversation with him. At the same time, she was escaping being questioned by him, which could only be a good thing. She didn't know what information DI Reid was privy to.

Preoccupied with her thoughts, Andie climbed onto her bike and headed for home. She was already half a mile down the road before she realized it was raining.

Damn, she really could have used her jacket.

This really wasn't her day.

CHAPTER TEN

DESSIE

essie and Grayson looked at each other with raised eyebrows after Andie had left the break-fast room.

"Do I have something on my face?" Grayson asked, touching his mouth and cheeks. "Do I look weird today?"

"No." Dessie laughed. "You look perfect, as always." She glanced down, feeling her face flush. She really needed a better filter in Grayson's presence.

Grayson smoothed things over by joining in her laughter. "I wasn't imagining it, was I? She just stared at me for ages."

"She did. But I thought she was a little off today, anyway. More than usual. She always has this intense look in her eyes. She seems a little too serious for a girl her age." Dessie ordinarily wouldn't have said something like that about an employee, but she welcomed the change of subject and the distraction from showing her feelings for Grayson.

"Today her gaze seemed even more penetrating. I don't want to speak ill of her. She is a very nice young woman, hardworking, very diligent. I much prefer working along-side her to working with Tara, who is a bit of a chatterbox. And, I mean, I sprung the extra hours on her with no warning, and I'm very grateful she took that on. But today…it felt like every time I turned around she was there, staring at me."

"I know what you mean," Grayson agreed. "She kept barging in, asking questions she should know the answers to…it felt a bit intrusive. I don't mean to sound arrogant, but I think she's jealous."

"Jealous? What do you mean?"

"Well, the girl keeps looking at me like…you know, maybe she's into me. Supposedly, women find me attrac-tive," he said with a self-deprecating smile.

"Oh, I see, um…" Dessie stuttered. "I mean, she might…although, aren't you a bit old for her? Anyway, why would that make her jealous, just because…" Dessie trailed off. Then she realized what Grayson was getting at. "Oh! But we're just friends. There's nothing…um…" She didn't know where to look and busied herself with the zipper of her cardigan.

"She doesn't know that." Grayson shrugged.

Dessie was glad to hear a knock at the door at that moment. This conversation was getting way too uncom-fortable for her. "Come in," she called.

DI Reid entered the breakfast room. "The MacLeod lass let me in," he explained after greeting Dessie and Grayson.

Dessie pointed to a chair at their table, and Grayson introduced himself before asking, "Can I get you some-thing to drink, Inspector?"

DI Reid declined with a wave of his hand. "I expect my visit will be brief. Unfortunately, I have no news regarding Mrs. MacDonald, we…"

"I invited you here because *I* have news regarding Mrs. MacDonald," Dessie interrupted with an icy voice. DI Reid had barely sat down and already his condescending tone annoyed her. When she'd thought about the inspector in his absence, he'd seemed like a reasonable man. But in person, he really riled her up.

"In that case, I will have a cup of tea," DI Reid replied with a slight smile and sat back in his chair. His gaze fell on Dessie's foot, still resting on the chair next to him.

"I sprained my ankle last night," she explained in response to his questioning look.

Grayson went to the kitchen to make tea, but Dessie didn't want to wait any longer. "Let's get to the point. Since you didn't find it pertinent to investigate Mrs. MacDonald, I had to take care of the matter myself."

Inspector Reid sighed. "Please don't tell me you were spying on the old lady, Mrs. McKendrick."

"You left me no choice. You didn't want to believe that she had anything to do with my husband's or Nate Saunders's disappearances." Dessie lifted her chin and met the inspector's eyes. She'd thought they were brown, but now she noticed the green flecks. It would have made him attractive, if he hadn't had a condescending smile on his face.

"We have looked into Mrs. MacDonald, and we have made only two shocking discoveries. One, she used to get bad reviews from her guests for using powdered eggs, and two, she is partial to a Continental knitting style, which her church group tut-tutted about." He looked up as Grayson handed him a cup of tea. "Thank you." Grayson placed milk and sugar on the table.

Dessie waited until DI Read had stirred in two lumps of sugar and raised the cup to his lips, then said drily, "So you have yet to discover she's a devil worshipper."

The inspector snorted, and tea came out his nose. He coughed as he grabbed a handful of napkins from the center of the table to wipe his face.

"Yes, that's right," Dessie said smugly. "I followed Mrs. MacDonald into the woods last night, where she met up with a bunch of other women. They wore creepy robes with hoods pulled down over their faces, and they all had brooches in the shape of pentacles to fasten their robes. They danced around a fire, chanting, and then they sacrificed an animal. A sheep, I believe. They killed a sheep right in front of me."

DI Reid stared at her with big eyes.

"No, I didn't imagine it, Inspector. And Mrs. MacDonald was not the only person there I recognized. Rosa Simmonds, your receptionist, is part of this satanic cult, too."

DI Reid slowly put his cup of tea down. Then he looked questioningly at Grayson, who was still standing.

Grayson raised his hands, showing his palms. "I didn't see anything. I just found Dessie injured in the woods. But I believe her. I mean, why would she make something like that up?"

"How did you injure your foot, Mrs. McKendrick?" Dessie saw pity in DI Reid's eyes. "Did you maybe hit your head, too? Maybe you passed out and…"

"I didn't hallucinate this. I saw the women in the forest. My ankle injury happened afterward, as I ran away."

"Do you really expect me to believe that Mrs. MacDonald, the frail old woman with a walking stick, hiked into the woods at night and danced around a fire?"

"I know how it sounds," Dessie said impatiently. "But it's the truth. I don't know if they are devil worshippers or what kind of pagan ritual they were performing. I only know they had the pentacle brooches, and they sacrificed an animal and chanted. That's not normal behavior. I was scared, to tell you the truth. And if they are sacrificing animals, it's not too far-fetched that they would sacrifice humans now, is it?"

"Come on, now, Mrs. McKendrick." DI Reid's expression changed from amused to annoyed. "A couple of elderly ladies from Tarbet overpowering grown men and dragging them into the woods to sacrifice them to the devil?"

When the inspector said it, Dessie had to admit that it did sound rather ridiculous. "But I know what I saw," she said in exasperation. "I didn't make it up."

DI Reid studied her for a moment. He must have seen something in her eyes that made him decide she believed what she was saying. His voice was soft when he said, "I believe you saw something. But most likely, it wasn't what you thought. I know you're still distressed about your husband's disappearance, and what happened to Nate Saunders brought it all back to you. I understand that. Under the circumstances… could it be that you misinterpreted what you saw?"

Dessie shook her head stubbornly.

DI Reid sighed. "You say you saw Rosa there? Well then, let's ask her what she and the other women were doing. Maybe there's a very simple explanation."

"What simple explanation could there be?" Grayson interjected. Dessie gave him a grateful smile. This didn't seem to escape the inspector. For some reason, though, it seemed to displease him.

His soft, friendly expression disappeared, and he said stiffly, "Explain to me again how you're involved in this, Mr. DuMont?"

"Dessie called me after she took a tumble in the woods. I went looking for her and carried her to the car. Then I drove her to the hospital."

"So you haven't seen any alleged devil worshippers." It was more of a statement than a question.

"No," Grayson had to admit. "I didn't. But if Dessie says she saw…"

"All right, thank you," the inspector interrupted him. "That will be all." He stood up.

Dessie panicked. "You're just going to leave? But…what are you going to do about this?"

"Like I said, I'm going to ask Rosa—"

"No!" Dessie cut him off. "She'll just deny it, won't she? She'll come up with some excuse. And then they'll know we're on to them and try to cover their tracks."

"What tracks?" Now it was the inspector's turn to sound exasperated. "Are there any? Is there any proof of what you claim to have seen? If so, then let's go into the forest and find the place where all this supposedly took place. If there is blood evidence, I'll have it tested."

Dessie stayed silent for a minute. She tried hard not to cry. "I don't think I could find the place again," she admitted. "And I can't walk. But I could tell you roughly where it is…"

DI Reid looked down at her for what seemed like ages. Dessie felt very uncomfortable. Finally, he said, "Can you show me on a map?"

"Maybe. We do have those Argyll Forest Park leaflets with hiking trails for our guests." Dessie looked up at the inspector with renewed hope.

"Okay, then. Try to narrow down the area, scan the map, and email it to me. Park rangers are combing the forest, anyway. I'll have them pay special attention to the area you identify. If there are remains of a fire…or of a slaughtered sheep…they should find them. Then I can examine the scene of the…ritual…further. Sound good?"

Dessie chewed her lower lip indecisively. That

sounded…laborious. She hadn't actually thought about *how* her new information would aid the investigation.

Only when he mentioned talking to Rosa had Dessie realized she had no proof, and alerting the group of women in that way would allow them to get rid of any evidence and make them more careful.

And there was something else she hadn't considered. Last night, she'd been full of adrenaline, and then she'd been far too exhausted to think about it. Today, she had enjoyed being taken care of by Grayson far too much.

Everything had been a distraction, and she hadn't thought about what her discovery meant regarding Connor's disappearance.

Had these women really killed her husband as part of a satanic ritual?

"Mrs. McKendrick?" DI Reid interrupted her thoughts. "Can you do that, or should I talk to Rosa and get to the bottom of it that way?"

"No," Dessie said firmly. "You're right. The park rangers should find the spot, and then you can collect the evidence. There was a big boulder that served as a sort of sacrificial altar. The animal's blood should be on there, and if they also used it for—" Dessie swallowed. "Human sacrifice, then maybe you'll find traces of Nate's and…Connor's blood." She squeezed her eyes shut and took a deep breath. She suddenly felt very sick. "I'll email you the map, Inspector." She forced herself to look at him.

DI Reid put a card on the table. "My email address is on here."

He said goodbye and turned to leave, but he looked back and added, "And Mrs. McKendrick? Please refrain from spying on anyone. Leave the investigation to the police, okay?"

Dessie just nodded absently, still thinking about what her new theory meant.

DI Reid seemed to hesitate, then pulled a pen out of his jacket pocket. "You know what? I'm going to write my private phone number on the back of the card. Before you get any ideas about investigating on your own and get hurt again or something, call me, please."

After the inspector left, Grayson said, "Why don't I cook for us tonight? I make a good lasagna, if you're in the mood for Italian?"

Before the conversation with the inspector, Dessie would have happily agreed. But now, all she could think about was Connor. She felt guilty that she had enjoyed having Grayson pay so much attention to her.

If she was right—and she knew what she had seen!— then that would mean bad things for Connor. Of course, she had always known that her husband couldn't be alive anymore. She'd never believed Inspector Murray's reassurances that he had merely run away. Connor would never have done that to her, so that meant something terrible must have happened to him.

But there had always been a tiny spark of hope in her heart. She had spent ten years trying to find out what happened to Connor, and now, as she was getting close, she realized that this hope had to die.

"I don't really have an appetite," she barely managed to get out. "Maybe I'll feel like eating later, but please don't go to any trouble. I'll find something in the fridge. I've already taken up too much of your time today."

When Grayson started to protest, she blurted, "I'm going to my room now, to look at maps and identify the area for the search. Then I think I'll lie down. I just realized how tired I am."

She turned away from Grayson so he wouldn't see her tear-filled eyes. When she tried to get up, he was immediately by her side to help her. Dessie shrugged him off. "It's okay, I'll manage."

She limped to the door. Then she turned around. "Oh, but if you don't mind, could you stay in the B&B and check in guests when they arrive? Room four is still available if someone comes without a reservation."

It bothered her to ask Grayson for help, but she really needed a few hours of peace and quiet.

"Of course." Grayson stepped to her side and put a hand on her shoulder. "If you change your mind about dinner, let me know. If I can help in any other way, I will. Just say the word. I'm here for you, Dessie."

Dessie just nodded, a big lump in her throat. She awkwardly pushed open the door with her crutch and said nothing when Grayson held it open for her. She then hobbled to the office to pick up a map. Tucking it under her arm, she made her way to her room.

Once she'd firmly shut the door behind her, she placed the map on her desk, tossed the crutches aside, and flopped down on the bed.

She buried her face in a pillow and allowed herself to cry for Connor.

≈

WISPY CLOUDS of mist floated over the loch, softening the dramatic orange and purple of the evening sky.

Dessie soaked in the view as she crossed the lawn in front of Rowardennan Youth Hostel toward the jetty, two Styrofoam cups of coffee in her hands. It wasn't just the picturesque scenery; it was Connor, who turned around and smiled at her.

He was the only person on the jetty, because they were still much too early. The water taxi wouldn't depart for another half an hour. They had been waiting outside the youth hostel for hours, eating sweets from the vending machine in the entrance area and drinking the terrible coffee sold at the reception desk.

When an older gentleman had tried to engage them in a conversation, they'd decided to go to the jetty. They enjoyed their own company and didn't feel they needed anyone else. Long-distance walking on the West Highland Way was a rather lonely affair; sometimes hours passed before they ran into anyone else. Dessie kind of enjoyed having Connor all to herself, and he seemed to feel the same way.

Connor had carried the backpacks to the jetty, and Dessie had volunteered to pick up more coffee.

Connor lit a cigarette with the silver Zippo lighter she had given to him as a present, blowing smoke casually toward Loch Lomond, where it disappeared into the mist. With a sweet grin, he accepted the coffee cup she held out to him. Then he kissed her to say thank you. He used any excuse to kiss her, but they were on their honeymoon, after all. Dessie got butterflies every time, as if it were their first kiss.

When the water taxi arrived, no passengers from the other side of the loch disembarked, but Dessie and Connor were not the only ones on their way back to Tarbet. They were joined by three young couples who, Dessie assumed, had also chosen Rowardennan Youth Hostel for overnight accommodation without booking in advance—and had, like Connor and Dessie, been told that there were no beds available.

The next part of the trail was supposed to be rather challenging, and the next place to stay was in Inversnaid—a good four-hour hike away. So the detour to Tarbet made sense. This was the last taxi to depart that day, and it would arrive in Tarbet fairly late.

Tarbet Hotel appeared out of the mist in front of them just as the sun set behind them. The mountain scenery disappeared in the night sky. But the hotel was full as well, and Dessie and Connor made their way through a dark and rainy Tarbet in search of somewhere to spend the night.

"Sorry, I just gave away the last room," a landlord said to them. Dessie realized it must have gone to one of the other couples in the water taxi.

"Quick," she joked. "This is now a competition."

Giggling, they ran up the street, heavy backpacks jiggling, away from the other couple walking a few hundred yards behind them.

They soon stopped laughing, though, when they got the same response everywhere they went. "Sorry, we are fully booked."

It started to pour as they reached the end of the main road. They'd knocked on what felt like every door in the village. For the first time during their honeymoon, their mood was less than stellar.

Even the wet campground in Easter Drumquhassle after the first leg of the hike had been better. They had been exhausted, cold, and shivering. It had been a major hassle to put the tent up, but in the end, they'd crawled happily into their sleeping bags. It had been kind of cozy.

The thought of pitching a tent in the pouring rain on the side of the road seemed too depressing to Dessie to contemplate now, but it looked like that would be their last recourse.

When the lady at the last B&B—according to the map, the road continued to Arrochar, but that was still a few miles away—attempted to slam the door in their faces, Dessie stopped her. "Please, we've been everywhere. There are no rooms available in this village. Do you have any idea where we could stay?"

The woman studied them with pity in her eyes. "Hmm, maybe there's a room available at the Thistle Inn, Mrs.

MacDonald's place. She doesn't have a sign on the main road, and it's a little hidden at the edge of the village, so not a lot of tourists stumble across it. You might be in luck."

They followed the woman's directions, and when the owner of the Thistle Inn opened the door and told them she had a spare room, Dessie was almost tempted to hug her. But when Mrs. MacDonald showed them the room, Dessie was glad she hadn't followed that impulse.

The woman looked creepy, with her tangled black hair sticking up from her head and her big, yellow teeth. Her lips were bright red, which accentuated the wrinkles around her mouth and probably made her look older than she was. Her teeth protruded a bit like a horse's, and they were smeared with lipstick. She stooped over her walking stick.

The room had old-fashioned furnishings. The bed looked as if nobody had slept in it since the 1960s. At least that was when the orange and brown pattern of the faded and dusty crocheted coverlet had last been in fashion.

Dessie decided she could stand disgusting sheets; if it was really bad, she could always use her sleeping bag. The room didn't seem heated, but at least it was dry. She couldn't wait to have a hot shower and then get into fresh clothes.

Dessie opened the door that she assumed led to the bathroom, but it was merely a closet with worm-ridden wood. "Where is the bath?"

"Oh, it's in the hallway. We share," the old woman croaked. Dessie followed her. Her eyes widened when she saw the old lady's personal toiletries lined up above the sink. She had stayed in places where guests shared a bathroom, but she had never heard of guests sharing with the landlady.

The only good thing to say about the bathroom was

that it looked fairly clean. The toilet cover, toilet roll holder, and bathmats were crocheted in shades of pink, brown, and orange, the colors clashing with the avocado-green bathroom tiles.

When the old woman turned her hunched back to them, Dessie grinned at Connor, and he winked back at her. Dessie relaxed and took Connor's hand as they followed the old lady back into the hallway. They could already joke about it—this wasn't so bad.

"What time would you like breakfast tomorrow?" Mrs. MacDonald asked.

Dessie didn't even want to know what the woman's kitchen looked like. She almost shivered with disgust, thinking about eating anything prepared by those bony fingers with long black hair on the knuckles.

"Eight o'clock would be great," Connor answered. "But all we need is a box of cereal, and we'll help ourselves. We're pretty low maintenance."

Dessie squeezed his hand gratefully. He probably knew what she was thinking.

Mrs. MacDonald jotted down their names in a black notebook she retrieved from the deep folds of her voluminous black skirt. "Married? A bit young for that, aren't you?" she commented when Dessie automatically told her they were on their honeymoon.

"You're from Edinburgh, then?" the woman continued.

"Huh? How did you know that?" Dessie's eyes widened.

"Because you're on your honeymoon."

Connor and Dessie looked at each other with raised eyebrows.

Mrs. MacDonald explained, "Newlyweds from Edinburgh traditionally visit Tarbet on their honeymoon. It puts the marriage under a good star."

"We didn't know that," Connor said, smiling at Dessie.

"We hadn't actually intended to come to Tarbet," she added, secretly thrilled about the romantic coincidence.

The old woman twisted the corners of her mouth into what could be interpreted as a smile. "Goodnight, then."

After she closed the door behind her, Dessie and Connor looked at each other and waited until they couldn't hear the walking stick hitting the floor anymore. They both burst out laughing.

"Thank you for suggesting cereal for breakfast. I was already afraid to find one of her warts in my scrambled eggs," Dessie finally managed to say when she got her breath back.

Connor laughed. "I bet she likes to share her bathroom with the guests because she never uses it herself."

"Well, let's hope the water is hot. Shall we use the bathroom together?"

"Kinky." Connor wriggled his eyebrows.

"Ew," Dessie said, giggling. "Not in there. And not in here, either. It's gross. No, I just don't want to be in this house by myself. It's kind of creepy, don't you think?"

They got ready for bed together. Back in their room, they spread one sleeping bag on the bed and used the other as a blanket. They snuggled—and in the end got over how gross the B&B was as passion took over. When Dessie fell asleep, warm and content in Connor's arms, she wasn't thinking about their accommodations or Mrs. MacDonald anymore.

THE FIRST THING Dessie noticed when she opened her eyes the next morning was the yellowed floral wallpaper peeling off the wall. Then she realized she was cold. She turned over. Connor wasn't in bed, and the sleeping bag had slipped to the floor. She pulled it back up. A glance at the alarm clock on the nightstand told her it wasn't seven o'clock yet.

She tried to go back to sleep, but the need to use the bathroom grew stronger. She'd assumed Connor was using it, because where else would he have gone? When he hadn't reappeared ten minutes later, Dessie got up and quickly threw on some clothes. She went into the hallway and impatiently knocked on the bathroom door.

No answer. Tentatively, she turned the knob. There was no one in the bathroom. She really had to pee, so she used the toilet and quickly washed her hands and brushed her teeth.

Connor still wasn't in their room when she got back. Uncertain, she went back to the hallway and stood there, listening to the silence. Finally, she knocked at the door that Mrs. MacDonald had pointed out was the kitchen.

It was dark and empty. It didn't look as if Mrs. MacDonald was up yet. Dessie didn't dare go through the kitchen into her landlady's private quarters. Instead, she went back to the front door, looked out, saw no one, then returned to the room. She opened the window and called out, "Connor?"

She wondered if he had gone outside to have a smoke. Maybe he was out of cigarettes and had gone to find a shop? Would anything be open this early?

Dessie grew more and more concerned as the minutes ticked by. To keep busy, she rolled up the sleeping bags and put the few things they had unpacked yesterday back into their backpacks. Connor didn't seem to have taken anything with him.

By eight o'clock, she was frantic.

She went into the kitchen, where she found Mrs. MacDonald. "Have you seen my husband?"

The old woman just stared at her with dead eyes. She

wore the same clothes as the night before and had the same red, smudged lipstick.

It seemed to Dessie as if Mrs. MacDonald took forever to reply.

"No," she finally said. "He's gone."

CHAPTER ELEVEN

ANDIE

When Andie set off to work in a last-minute dash, she realized how cold it was and went to grab her jacket. As she opened the closet, she remembered she'd left it at the B&B the day before.

She quickly surveyed her options. Andie's mom was even more petite than her, so none of her jackets would fit. Her dad's coats seemed much too big. There had to be jackets she had left at home packed away somewhere, but she was in a hurry and quickly threw on her cape.

As she was cycling to the B&B, she regretted that decision. The hood was so wide that it kept falling into her eyes and obstructing her vision.

Luckily, there wasn't a lot of traffic at six in the morning, so she survived unscathed and arrived at the B&B on time.

Andie unlocked the door, stepped into the corridor, and listened. It was very quiet. None of the guests seemed to be up this early. There was no sign of Dessie and, thankfully, Grayson was nowhere to be seen, either.

Hopefully, today she could finally talk to Dessie about the encounter in the woods, she thought, as she hung the cape on the coat rack. There were a few things she needed to explain to Dessie. She wasn't sure if her boss had tried to avoid the conversation so far, or if it was a coincidence that she hadn't been able to catch her alone yesterday.

Maybe Dessie had wanted to talk to the inspector first? Andie wished she'd had a chance to listen in on their conversation. She sighed. She'd talk to Dessie today, come what may. But she certainly wouldn't do it in front of Grayson.

Despite her efforts, she still hadn't "seen" anything about him, but that hadn't made her feel any better about the American. She had a feeling that Grayson would get in Andie's way, for whatever reason, and her intuition usually proved right.

Unfortunately, most people weren't convinced by that. They needed tangible proof. Andie had learned that lesson many times over.

Dessie wouldn't believe her if she explained her visions and her feelings regarding Grayson. Which left Andie with no other course of action but to answer her calling without trying to explain herself to Dessie. After all, it was for her boss's own good.

Andie turned on the light in the hallway. The light reflected on the metal of the brooch on her cape.

She took the brooch off and put it in the pocket of her jacket, which was still on the coat rack where she'd left it yesterday.

Andie mentally scolded herself for not thinking about removing the precious item sooner. It would be careless to leave it out for all the guests—and Dessie—to see.

Mrs. MacDonald would kill her if she knew.

CHAPTER TWELVE

DESSIE

Dessie's foot was less swollen and didn't hurt as much. She still had to use her crutches, though. Grayson didn't want her to walk around at all, insisting that she should rest and that he'd take care of her.

Dessie ignored him and hobbled down the corridor to get the mail. Even though she told him off for coddling her, she was secretly pleased about how protective he seemed. It warmed her heart to know he cared about her.

Her mood changed when her gaze fell upon the coat rack.

A shiver ran down Dessie's spine when she recognized the large black cape.

Dessie looked around. No one was close by, so she leaned one of her crutches against the wall and hesitantly touched the fabric. The wide hood with the velvet lining... this was unmistakably one of the cloaks the women in the woods had worn.

It felt unreal to see it here, in her B&B, like she was the victim of a sick prank or something.

Could the cape belong to one of her guests? The only women currently staying had checked in yesterday evening, so it didn't look as if they'd have anything to do with it. Then there were Val and Nicole…

She remembered the short person who had caught her spying on the group. Had there been long dark hair spilling out of the hood? Dessie couldn't be sure anymore. It had all gone so fast.

It could have been Nicole, who was petite and brunette, but…she wasn't from here. It made little sense that she would be part of a group of local women doing god only knew what in the woods. And who, in Dessie's opinion, were responsible for Nate's disappearance.

Surely Nicole wasn't mixed up in this. But no, she wouldn't have involved the police, instead finding another excuse for her boyfriend's absence. Plus, Dessie couldn't believe that Nicole was that good of an actress.

As Dessie fingered the silky cape, she noticed it was hanging on top of a coarser fabric—another jacket. That struck her as odd; after all, there was plenty of space on the coat rack. She pushed the cape aside to examine the jacket.

It hit Dessie all of a sudden.

This was Andie's jacket.

Her employee was also petite and dark-haired.

Following an impulse, she searched the pockets of the jacket. When her fingers came across something hard and sharp, she wasn't even surprised. Nevertheless, her breath caught in her throat when she opened her hand and saw what she had pulled out: the pentacle brooch with the amethyst thistle.

Dessie stared at it until she heard a door slam.

She quickly slipped the brooch back into the pocket, picked up her crutch, and opened the front door in a daze.

Absentmindedly, she opened the mailbox, took out the stack of letters, and jammed them under her arm.

She just dumped the mail on her desk in the office

without looking at it, then hobbled quickly toward the kitchen, where Grayson was busy with the grocery list.

Before she got there, the door to room number six opened, and Andie stepped out.

They both stopped in their tracks and stared at each other for a moment. Just as Andie opened her mouth, Dessie muttered, "Sorry," and pushed past as fast she could on her crutches. Andie, who was struggling with an arm full of sheets, didn't stop her.

Dessie was panting by the time she made it to her seat in the kitchen.

Grayson closed the fridge door and wrote something down on a notepad. When he looked up again, he noticed Dessie's distress. His eyebrows drew together. "Are you okay? Did you overdo it? I told you I could—"

"Not here," Dessie interrupted him. She got up and opened the porch door, gesturing for Grayson to follow her.

"What—?" he began, but Dessie shushed him.

She closed the sliding door and checked to be sure the windows of the guest rooms facing the garden were closed.

When she turned her attention back to Grayson, he seemed very concerned. "What's wrong? Shouldn't you be sitting down?" He pointed her toward the porch swing.

Dessie dismissed him with a wave of her hand.

"She's one of them," she said excitedly. "Andie. She's one of the women I saw in the woods the other night."

"What? How did you find out?" She was grateful that Grayson didn't sound skeptical, just concerned.

She told him about the brooch.

"Aha. I knew there was something wrong with that girl. She's so...intense. She gives me the creeps," Grayson admitted.

"I didn't notice it before, but since you mentioned something similar yesterday…"

Dessie fell silent. She abruptly realized how exhausted she felt, so she headed to the swing to sit down after all. Grayson took her arm without asking and helped her settle. "Thanks. What are we going to do now?" She looked up at him. "Do you think I should call Inspector Reid?"

"I'm not sure it would make any difference to his investigation. You saw the brooch on the women in the woods, and now you've discovered that one that looks the same belongs to Andie. I think he would question whether it really is the same piece of jewelry. He'd suggest that we ask her about it, and then we'd have the same issue as we would have had if he'd confronted Rosa."

Dessie sank back into the swing cushion. The adrenaline of finding the brooch had fizzled out, and now she was just tired.

Grayson was right. The inspector might not find the brooch and Andie's connection important enough to investigate her. The brooch in itself wasn't any evidence at all.

But Dessie could feel that it was important.

There were connections forming all around Dessie like a web, and she didn't think it was a coincidence.

Val and Sam had stayed at her B&B. She herself had sent Nate and Nicole to Mrs. MacDonald. Andie had just started working here a few weeks ago.

"I overheard Andie talking on the phone earlier. I think she spoke with someone called Fionna and said she'd come to the meeting tonight. What if it's the same group you encountered the other night?"

Dessie looked at him with interest. "Did Andie mention any details? Where is the meeting taking place, and when?"

He shook his head and stayed silent for a moment. "It sounded to me as if Fionna was worried Andie wouldn't make it in time. Maybe she told her she'd have to work more because of your injury? Andie assured her she'd get there in plenty of time because she could take her mom's car."

Dessie's eyes widened. "Then we need to follow her. Maybe it's another one of those…ritualistic…meetings? And then we can call the police. If DI Reid catches them in a satanic rite…"

"Yes, but didn't he tell you not to spy on anyone anymore?" Grayson interrupted her.

"It is my only option. He won't believe me if I just tell him about it. I have to make him see it with his own eyes." When Grayson didn't reply, Dessie added gruffly. "You don't have to help me. I'll just do it by myself." She tried to stand up but couldn't get out of the deep seat of the swing by herself. Annoyed, Dessie swore.

"Calm down," Grayson said, amused. "Of course, I'll help you. You can't drive, can you?"

"I'll be fine," she said defiantly.

"Hey, listen to me." He put his hands on her shoulders and looked at her until she met his gaze. "I said I'm here for you, remember?"

As Dessie looked into his beautiful brown eyes, the thought occurred to her that she could let all of this go. She could let the past be the past, end the obsession, let the police handle everything where Nate was concerned…and just lose herself in his eyes.

She swallowed. "All right, thank you."

Grayson smiled. "We'll wait until Andie gets off work and then drive my rental car to her house. You know where she lives, right?"

Dessie nodded. "She stays with her parents. I have the address on file."

"Good, we'll follow her. Let's see where the little witch leads us."

He probably meant it as a joke, but it sounded a bit mean to Dessie. Threatening, even. She brushed the thought aside. After all, she was grateful to have Grayson's support.

A few hours later, Grayson and Dessie were parked on the street where Andie's parents lived. They didn't have to wait long before Andie exited the house and got into an old red Fiat.

Grayson started the engine, and they followed Andie at a safe distance down the road to Arrochar. Andie passed through the village and chose a route in the direction of the Arrochar Alps. The road wound its way through the Argyll Forest, up the mountains.

Twenty minutes later, Andie turned onto a dirt track. Grayson continued on the main road.

"Hey, what are you doing?" Dessie asked, scared they'd lose Andie.

"It's too conspicuous if I turn right behind her," Grayson said reassuringly. He turned around at the next opportunity, drove back, and turned down the dirt road.

Dessie had to admit she was a little impressed by how confident Grayson was. He seemed to be a natural at this. The narrow dirt road let to an area where a few cars were parked. She spotted the red Fiat. "There!" she shouted excitedly.

They left their car next to the others and found a little footpath leading from the parking area into the woods.

Dessie had trouble with her crutches, but Grayson helped her patiently. She wondered if he heard her heart pounding. What if one of the women arrived after them and came up behind them? Or if any of the women had to get something out of her car? They would have questions for Dessie and Grayson, and what excuse could they give? Could they be in danger?

Grayson didn't seem nervous or in a hurry at all. Dessie was glad he was by her side, especially because it was getting dark. It was too early for the sun to set—maybe there was a storm brewing.

The path led to a cabin. There was light on inside.

Grayson indicated to Dessie that they should leave the path and sneak around the cabin to the back. Maybe they could look through a window undetected.

Dessie nodded, but an inconspicuous approach with crutches proved to be difficult. Grayson got to the window before her and peered through the pane. There was a water trough underneath, and he had to lean over it.

Dessie caught up to him and attempted to get a look in as well. Grayson helped her, and she could just catch a glimpse over the high windowsill.

Several women sat on the floor in two rows facing each other. In the middle, between the two rows, was a long wooden board.

Dessie recognized Mrs. MacDonald and Rosa again. They were standing in the back of the cabin, next to what looked like a tub. They pulled something out of the water and spread it out on the board.

Dessie strained her eyes, but she couldn't quite make out what it was. Wet blankets? Or something more sinister? She shuddered to think what else it could be.

Then the women sitting on the floor in front of the board proceeded to stomp on the wet stuff with their feet. At first it seemed random, but then they started to sing, and their feet moved in rhythm to the song.

It had to be another ritual, like the animal sacrifice in the woods.

The women really got into it, kicking their feet wildly at the thing on the board. Dessie's throat closed up. It was so bizarre…primal even. It had to be an ancient pagan ritual of some kind.

The words of the song sounded Gaelic, just like the

chants Dessie had heard in the forest. There was a repetitive chorus that made the song quite catchy.

Rosa and Mrs. MacDonald seemed like high priestesses, standing at the head of the board, conducting the women.

Dessie could only see the backs of those sitting in the row underneath the window, but she could make out the faces of the women on the other side. There was Andie, next to a very attractive blond. Dessie almost jumped when she spotted Tara, who had been her employee for several summers, and who had told her she couldn't help out this year but suggested Andie as a replacement.

It took Dessie a while to spot the red-haired curvy young woman she had seen in the woods, but eventually she noticed her behind the tub. Dessie pressed herself against the trough, leaning forward even further until she could see what the young woman was doing. She added something to the tub. Her lips moved, and she seemed highly focused on her task. The chanting women didn't appear to distract her.

Dessie almost fell into the trough, but Grayson held her steady. "Careful!"

"Look," Dessie whispered. "Look at what the red-haired girl is doing behind the…I guess it's a cauldron."

Grayson pressed his face against the window, turning his head to get a better look.

"A witch," he whispered. "She is doing some sort of spell. Son of a gun, you were right. These women are witches."

Dessie whispered, "I need to get out of earshot so I can call Inspector Reid."

Grayson nodded without taking his eyes off what was going on inside the cabin.

Dessie moved slowly away, careful not to trip on the uneven ground. She stopped next to a large tree, leaned a crutch against the wide trunk, and stepped behind it to make the call to the inspector.

As she listened to the ringing, she peeked out from behind the trunk in the direction of the cabin. Everything looked the same. In the semi-dark, she saw the outline of the wooden structure with the window as a yellow rectangle and Grayson's silhouette in front of it.

"Hello?" DI Reid answered.

"This is Dessie McKendrick," she said quietly. "We've caught the devil worshippers in the act, and you'll have to come to..." To what? What would the police do in such a situation? "Arrest them," she finished, somewhat at a loss.

The inspector was silent for a moment. "Okay, what do you mean, caught in the act? What crime are they committing?"

"Well, I don't know, but they are in the middle of some sort of bizarre satanic ritual again." Dessie became impatient and peered around the tree. Nothing had changed.

"Are you telling me you came across a group of women dancing around a bonfire? Again? The park rangers haven't found the place you described and—"

"No, not the same place, and not a bonfire," Dessie interrupted him. "This time, they're in a cabin. In the Arrochar Alps. There's a turn onto a dirt track about twenty minutes past Arrochar…" She gave him directions, but DI Reid didn't seem in a hurry to follow her directions. "Listen," she urged him. "When you see it with your own eyes, you'll find these rituals disconcerting, too, and understand what I mean. You have to come here. Fast."

DI Reid sighed, but curiosity got the better of him, she guessed, and he finally told her he was on his way.

Dessie hobbled back to Grayson with the good news. They took turns watching the women, mainly to ensure that nobody would come out of the cabin and see them. The ritual continued as before, and it didn't get any more interesting. As it was quite tiring to press against the trough and the window, Dessie didn't mind resting in between turns.

When the wet…piece of cloth, she hoped…was pulled off the board, Dessie noticed the board had grooves in it. New bits of wet stuff were pulled from the tub, placed on the board, and the whole thing started all over again with the first song.

Dessie was somewhat relieved. It looked as if the women wouldn't stop soon with their devilish activities, and the inspector had enough time to get here. But she was quite tired from all the excitement, her foot hurt again, and she just wanted this to be over with.

Once DI Reid saw all this, he would have to investigate Mrs. MacDonald and her group of…witches? Finally, she saw a dark figure climbing up the footpath. Dessie nudged Grayson, whose turn it was to look through the window.

The person was tall. Even so, it could be another devil worshipper coming late to the party. Dessie's heart almost leaped into her throat.

Then she recognized the man in the dusky light—the slate clouds had dissipated without a drop of rain. It was DI Reid.

When he reached them, Dessie didn't speak, just pointed at the window.

The inspector peered inside. Dessie got very impatient as she waited for him to turn around. She had to bite her lip not to say "I told you so."

When he did turn away from the window, she was satisfied that the equanimous expression had been wiped off his face. He looked more than a little disturbed.

"See," Dessie whispered excitedly. "Do you believe me now?"

"Hmm," DI Reid replied. Then he walked to the door. Dessie limped after him. "What are you going to do?"

He turned around. "What do you think?" he asked, his voice a normal volume. "I'm going to knock on the door, go in, and ask what's going on."

"But…" Dessie's jaw dropped. She almost tripped over her own crutches as she tried to catch up with the inspector. "Isn't that dangerous? Aren't you going to call for backup or something? Who knows what they'll do to you...to us…"

DI Reid looked at her with raised eyebrows. "I think I can handle whatever the women in the cabin are throwing at me, Mrs. McKendrick."

Before she could protest again, the inspector had already knocked and walked through the door. Stunned, Dessie looked at Grayson, who just shrugged.

Not wanting to miss anything, she followed the inspector into the cabin.

CHAPTER THIRTEEN

ANDIE

A ndie was getting tired. Her legs and feet were aching. She hadn't been part of this activity often lately, and her muscles weren't used to it.

When DI Reid entered the cabin, the interruption wasn't entirely unwelcome. Andie stopped what she was doing immediately, but a few of the other women were so focused on the task that it took them a while to notice what was going on. When more and more singing voices died down, the last of the rapt women stopped their enthusiastic chanting and treading.

Everyone stared in the direction of DI Reid. Then all eyes went to Mrs. MacDonald and Rosa. Heads moved yet again in the other direction, when Dessie McKendrick stormed into the cabin on crutches, closely followed by Grayson DuMont. It was a bit like they were watching a tennis match.

Penny Reid was the first to say something. "Hi, little brother!"

Inspector Reid gave her a curt nod. "Penny. What are you doing here, if you don't mind me asking?"

Dessie stared open-mouthed at the inspector. This tall

beauty with blond curls was related to the dark-haired police officer? They bore no resemblance to each other at all. "One of them is your sister?" Dessie forced the words out, then screwed up her face in annoyance. "Well, that explains it."

DI Reid turned to her, furrowing his brows. "It explains what, exactly?"

"Your unwillingness to investigate this cult." Dessie folded her arms in front of her chest, not an easy feat, considering she had to keep hold of her crutches. "You already knew about it, and…" Her expression changed from anger to fear. "Are you part of Nate's…and Connor's…" She stumbled back, running into Grayson, who put his hands on her shoulders to hold her steady.

"Wait a minute!" The inspector understood what she was getting at and raised his hands defensively. "There's no need to question my professional integrity or accuse me of who knows what. I had nothing to do with the disappearances. And as far as we know, neither did any of these ladies. One of them happens to be my sister, yes. One is a colleague. I know most of these women. Tarbet is a small place, and I grew up here."

Dessie swallowed visibly. "Well, you must admit that all these connections are a little suspicious," she said defiantly. "We followed Andie, my employee, here, because I found the brooch in her jacket, the same brooch I'd noticed on the women performing the pagan ritual in the woods."

Andie could feel Mrs. MacDonald's eyes on her. Uh-oh. She was in trouble.

"And I see Tara is here, who used to be in my employ, and who recommended Andie as her replacement," Dessie continued.

Mrs. MacDonald's gaze started to feel like a laser beam. Andie knew she'd have to answer a few questions later, and she was not looking forward to that.

"And then there is Mrs. MacDonald," Dessie's voice was booming by now. "The owner of the B&B where my husband disappeared from…and where Nate disappeared from, as well. You are the investigating officer in Nate's case, and then we find Rosa, your receptionist, here, and your sister. You can't blame me for—"

"Hang on." DI Reid tried to placate Dessie. "Yes, there seems to be a web of connections here, which isn't unusual in a small community, but we don't even know that whatever is going on here is connected to Nate or you and your husband at all. Let's find out what this is, first, shall we?" He held up a hand to stop Dessie from protesting and turned to the women. "Now, could someone please tell me what's going on?"

"We are a women's club, Declan, um, I mean DI Reid," Rosa said cheerfully. "We get together to do knitting and other traditional Highland crafts."

"A crafting club? Are you kidding me? You mean to tell me…" Dessie trailed off as her gaze went to the tartan shawls that had been hung to dry on one side of the cabin.

DI Reid noticed them, too. "I see."

Dessie flapped her arms, the ends of her crutches flying dangerously close to some of the other women's heads. "I don't. What are you supposedly making? Tartan cloth?"

"Mrs. McKendrick, you're not from here, so let me explain," Mrs. MacDonald croaked. "Waulking is a Scottish tradition. The cloth gets cleaned of impurities and the fibers mat together and shrink. The cloth turns soft, smooth, and waterproof. That's how our famous tartan cloth is traditionally made."

Dessie's gaze wandered over the women's bare feet and to the tub.

"This is how it is done," Mrs. MacDonald continued to explain. "By pounding the wet cloth with your feet."

Dessie bent awkwardly to touch the fabric on the

wooden board. Then she walked to the tub and fished a heavy piece of fabric out to inspect it. "It really is just cloth," she said incredulously. She looked a little relieved.

Then she sniffed the contents of the tub.

"Aha!" she exclaimed. "That smells funny. And you put some strange stuff in there." She pointed at Fionna. "I saw you do it."

"Herbs, certain...hmm...traditional ingredients, to help with the felting process." Mrs. MacDonald was nonplussed, whereas Fionna turned red in the face and kept her mouth shut.

Dessie looked around the cabin at the evidence for what Mrs. MacDonald had claimed they were doing. "But, but... The singing, those chants..."

The inspector cleared his throat. "I suppose what you heard were so-called waulking songs."

Rosa nodded. "Ye ken, Mrs. McKendrick, these are traditional songs women have been singing for centuries during this activity. Waulking is physically demanding and also monotonous, so women used to make up songs to make the work go faster and get into a nice rhythm."

"Like hiking songs," one woman interjected.

"Or like the US Army, where they march to songs. You see that in movies all the time," Penny spoke up. Everyone nodded in agreement.

Dessie's eyes were wide, almost panicked. "So you're really telling me this is just about a traditional Highland craft?"

Grayson, who must have noticed how distressed Dessie was, came to her and put an arm around her shoulders.

"Why yes, dearie, we're keeping old Highland traditions alive," Rosa exclaimed.

Dessie was silent for a moment. "But...what about the other night? In the woods? You danced around a fire! Sacrificed an animal! I saw it!" Her voice was hoarse and her eyes almost feverish. She shook off Grayson's arm and hobbled to the inspector. "What kind of knitting club does that? I'd like to hear an explanation for that!"

Silence in the cabin.

Andie, too, was dying to know what explanation Mrs. MacDonald or someone else would come up with. She didn't feel called upon to come up with one and draw attention to herself. She was in enough trouble already.

"Well, it's a wee bit…delicate, inspector," Mrs. MacDonald eventually offered. "We're all decent Christians, good churchgoing people…maybe not the young'uns, but ye ken how it is."

"So you did perform some sort of pagan ritual?" the inspector interrupted impatiently. His tone was serious, but Andie could see that the corners of his mouth were a little twitchy.

"We stick to old traditions…ancient traditions," Rosa admitted. That wasn't even a lie. "The cloth is blessed during a full-moon ceremony." Rosa's explanation sounded harmless, but then she had a talent for making everything seem harmless.

"And that involves slaughtering a sheep?" Dessie wasn't taken in by any of it. She turned to the inspector. "Surely there has to be a law against that. People can't be allowed to just go around killing animals for the fun of it."

DI Reid sighed. "You're right, of course."

Rosa had an answer ready. "I can assure you that everything went according to the law. Working for the police myself, I wouldn't dream of not complying with regulations. I'll happily bring all the veterinary records to work tomorrow, and we can discuss it in detail."

The inspector nodded. "That'll be fine. All right, we won't keep you from your task any longer." The inspector turned to leave. Dessie grabbed his arm. "But you can't…

Are you just going to leave…?" Then, with sheer incredulity in her voice, "Do you believe them?"

"Mrs. McKendrick," Inspector Reid said with a voice one might use to talk to a traumatized child. "What do you want me to do? You've seen what I've seen. The evidence for the waulking in this cabin. You heard their explanation. You have to admit that it is sound. It all fits. Now, tomorrow I will check that all went according to laws and regulations during this cloth-blessing ceremony. Other than that…" He shrugged his shoulders. "Do you see any evidence of wrongdoing? Anything the police should be involved in?"

Dessie opened her mouth, but nothing came out. Her fingers still clutched Inspector Reid's arm as she turned and searched Grayson's eyes. Grayson gently pulled her hand from the inspector's arm and helped her to the door. "Come on Dessie, let it go for now. We're going home." Dessie turned around with a helpless look but let him lead her outside.

DI Reid nodded goodbye to the women with an apologetic smile and left the cabin as well.

There was a long moment of tense silence before Mrs. MacDonald finally said, "Come on, carry on with the work. We've got a lot to do."

ANDIE FOLLOWED Dessie's double through the forest. The woman didn't seem to be in a hurry. In fact, Andie noticed now, she seemed much younger and more carefree, much happier, and nowhere near as hurried and hunched as the Dessie McKendrick Andie knew.

The Dessie double touched a tree trunk, closed her eyes, and took a deep breath. Andie stopped next to her and watched as a beatific smile spread across the young woman's face. When Dessie's double opened her eyes again, she fixed her gaze on Andie and her smile became even brighter. Then she chuckled lightly and skipped further along the forest path. Periodically, she looked around for Andie, who always followed her at the same distance.

As the path became steeper and stonier and the trees got smaller and fewer, Dessie's double's demeanor changed. She no longer smiled, and the look in her eyes turned from joy to fear. Her expression seemed anxious.

It appeared that she was trying to get away from Andie.

Dessie's double was getting more and more panicked. She moved faster, scrambling along the steep path. In the end, she looked like the Dessie of the present. Like a hunted animal. And Andie had become the hunter.

The chase through the forest seemed to continue endlessly. Dessie couldn't get away, but Andie also couldn't catch up to her.

Eventually, they reached the top of the mountain.

There was no escape for Dessie.

Shaking, she turned around to face Andie.

When their eyes met, Andie recognized more than fear in them.

Horror. Disappointment. A very painful realization.

Now Andie was able to shorten the distance between herself and Dessie's double. She approached the woman, who stood with her back to the precipice, gave her a push, and watched as Dessie fell with flailing arms over the ledge into a dark abyss.

Suddenly, Andie was no longer in the forest. Now she was standing on the shore of Loch Lomond. The sun had just risen, and a soft, diffuse light washed over the land-scape. The air was still, and the surface of the water was completely smooth.

It should have been a peaceful sight to behold, but

there was no peace inside Andie. There was nothing but a seething rage. Yet Andie knew on the outside she looked just as calm as the waters of the loch.

Nobody could fathom what darkness lay beneath the surface.

The peaceful sight of the loch was just as deceptive.

But Andie knew what was buried in its murky depths.

Connor McKendrick.

ANDIE SAT bolt upright in bed. She gasped for air, and her pulse raced. It took her a moment to realize where she was. In her old bedroom, in her parents' house.

Her mouth was dry.

Andie swung her legs out of bed and winced. Her muscles had never been so sore.

On bare feet, she plodded down the stairs to the kitchen where she took a glass from the dish drainer. She downed a glass of water and refilled it.

Her legs trembled, and she sat down at the kitchen table. What was she going to do?

WITH A QUEASY STOMACH, Andie set off for work the next morning. She didn't know how to face her boss, but she couldn't avoid the confrontation.

It was her job to be at the B&B—in more ways than one.

Dessie met her in the hallway, scowling even more than usual.

"Let's go into my office," she said curtly.

With a pounding heart, Andie followed her into the small room.

Dessie sat down on the swivel chair, and Andie had no

choice but to remain standing in front of her. She kneaded her hands together nervously and waited for Dessie to talk.

"Will you please close the door?"

Andie did as requested, turned back around, and met Dessie's rain-cloud-gray eyes.

At long last, Dessie began to talk. "I don't even know what to say to you, Andie. You work alongside me every day. And then I find out that you're one of *them*. I honestly feel betrayed. I mean, all this can't be a coincidence, and I have the very strong feeling that this group…that you… have something to do with Nate's disappearance… And I thought I was so close to finding out…finally…" Dessie lowered her head into her hands, took a few deep breaths, and looked up at Andie again.

"I'm giving you one chance to tell me the truth, Andie. What is this group you're involved with?"

"Um, it's a knitting and crafting club," Andie managed to say with a shaky voice.

She had been strongly advised to stick to that story, and she knew no further goodwill would be extended. She was lucky to have gotten away with a reprimand.

"A women's club. For knitting and crafting." Dessie's voice sounded flat. Like she had no more emotions to give. "That's it?"

Andie nodded. When Dessie said nothing again for a while, she filled the silence. "Well, you know, we don't just waulk. We do all kinds of things. It's just a…sort of women's club that keeps up local traditions. Old customs and stuff," she jabbered on.

"Andie." Dessie closed her eyes and seemed to be summoning up all her strength. "That's not all there is to it, is it? Mrs. MacDonald, what's up with her? I know she's behind Nate's disappearance. And Connor's." Dessie shook her head. "But you can't have anything to do with that.

You were only a little kid back then, weren't you? Nine or ten years old?"

Andie licked her dry lips. She was dying to tell Dessie what she knew. What she had seen. But she wasn't allowed to. Not now.

It pained her to see Dessie suffer like this. She didn't want to lie to her. After all, it was her job to help her, to protect her.

"Dessie," she burst out in desperation. "I can't tell you anything else right now, but please trust me…"

"I knew it!" Dessie jumped up, her crutches forgotten, her eyes glowing like dark coals. "You've got to tell me!" Dessie came closer, and Andie took a small step back until she stood with her back pressed against the door.

Andie shook her head. "I can't. But it's not what you think, really, Dessie. It's not what you think at all."

Dessie wasn't listening. "You have to talk to the inspector. Tell him everything. He thinks I'm crazy. Everybody thinks I'm crazy, but it's the truth, isn't it? Your women's group killed Nate, didn't they? And Connor?" Dessie grabbed Andie by the shoulders, her face only inches in front of her.

Tears sprang to Andie's eyes as she shook her head again. "No," she breathed. "We had nothing to do with it, I swear."

Dessie's brows drew together, her intense gaze boring into Andie. "What are you? Satanists? A coven or something?"

Andie groped behind her for the doorknob, finally found it, and the door popped open. Relieved, she took a step back and escaped Dessie's clinging grip. She would have liked to run away, but she had to stay. "We had nothing to do with what happened to your husband or Nate," she said more firmly now.

Dessie held her hands in the air for a moment, where

she had grabbed Andie by the shoulders. The flame that had flared up inside her seemed to fade out again as she lowered her arms and closed her eyes in resignation.

"Andie, I'm asking you one last time to tell me the truth. Please!" Desperation was written all over her face.

When Andie didn't say anything, Dessie's expression hardened. Her nostrils flared, and she opened her eyes.

"I can't," Andie whispered.

Dessie looked her up and down and then walked over to the desk, unlocked the top drawer, and took out a cash box. She lifted the coin tray, counted out a few bills that lay underneath, and stowed the box back in the desk.

She hobbled over to Andie and pressed the bills into her hand. "This will cover the days since your last paycheck, plus a little extra for overtime." In a tired voice, she added, "Now get out of here. I never want to see you here again."

Andie made a fist so that the bills crumpled in her sweaty hand. "Please don't fire me, Dessie."

Dessie let out a short, dry laugh without looking at her.

Andie took another hesitant step toward Dessie. "I can't tell you what we are—what I am—but I swear I had nothing to do with Nate and Connor's disappearance. Neither did Mrs. MacDonald or anyone else from the group. At least not directly—"

Dessie raised her hand, cutting Andie off. "Just go."

Now it was Andie's turn to sound as desperate as she felt. "You can't let me go. I have to stay here," she repeated. "Or you'll get hurt, and I'll…"

Dessie's eyes widened. "Is that supposed to be a threat?"

Andie unclenched her fist, not even noticing the damp, crumpled bills falling to the floor as she ran a hand through her hair. "No. Of course not. It is a warning, but I can't really tell you anything more."

Dessie looked like she had had enough, and Andie couldn't even blame her. How could she make her boss understand she had to trust her? How was she supposed to convince her to let her continue working here? She had to stay close to her at all costs.

"What do you think you're doing? Threatening me in my own home? I won't stand for it," Dessie said in a low voice.

"But that's not what I meant. You misunderstood me!"

Dessie narrowed her eyes. She sounded ice cold as she said, "I don't know what you did with Nate, with Connor. I don't know what you had to do with it. But I'm going to find out, if it's the last thing I do. Now get out!"

Andie went into the hallway and ran outside, letting the front door slam behind her, and jumped onto her bike. She was shaking and crying so hard, she almost crashed into a hedge.

She had wanted to do the right thing—but she had done it all wrong.

CHAPTER FOURTEEN

DESSIE

D essie listened to the sound of the front door slamming. She bent down as best as she could to pick up the crumpled bills. It took her a while, but eventually she had them gathered on her desk.

After she'd smoothed them out and put them back in the cash box, she took out her checkbook and wrote Andie a check for the same amount.

Her hands shook as she struggled to write legibly, but she persevered until she had the check in an envelope with Andie's address on it.

She put a stamp on it and added it to the stack of outgoing post.

Dessie was tired of her crutches, tired of looking and feeling vulnerable. She headed for the kitchen without them, but pain forced her to turn back. Grumbling, she limped back to the office and grabbed them.

When she finally made it to the kitchen, Grayson had set all the tables as per her instructions. She smiled at him, grateful to have at least one person she could rely on.

"You know how to fry eggs, don't you?" she asked hopefully.

"Yes, why?"

"Would you be willing to make breakfast for the guests this morning? I hate to ask, but I just fired Andie." She gestured with her crutches. "These stupid things make it a little difficult for me to move around the kitchen and breakfast room."

"Of course, Dessie." Grayson put a hand on her arm. "I'm happy to help, you know that." He eyed her critically. "Why don't you go back to bed for a bit? You look exhausted."

Dessie hesitated, and he brushed a wisp of hair from her face and tucked it behind her ear. Her first impulse was to recoil, but to her own surprise, she didn't. "But..." Dessie's mouth was dry, and she swallowed hard. "Don't you need me to tell you what to do?"

"Don't worry, I can manage on my own." Grayson gave her a bright smile. "If anyone orders something I don't know how to make, I'll just explain the situation to them. I'm sure they'll understand. In any case, I'll suggest to the guests that they order the Grayson special—I make a mean mushroom, bacon, and cheese omelet."

"Sounds delicious." Dessie yawned. Suddenly, she realized how tired she was. It felt like someone had put sacks of flour on her shoulders and the weight was pulling her toward the ground. Now she was grateful that the crutches were keeping her upright. "Yes, I guess I could use some more sleep."

Grayson nodded encouragingly and held the door open for her.

Dessie dragged herself out of the kitchen. But when she saw the door with the number three on it, she knew she wouldn't get any sleep. She took her keys out of her pocket and unlocked the room, which no one but her had entered since the B&B had opened.

The room had the usual effect on her. She felt simultaneously completely overwhelmed and also newly invigorated. She ignored the piles of things around her and immediately turned her attention to the wall.

It was plastered with photos, newspaper clippings, and other documents. Everything that had anything to do with Connor's disappearance and could be pinned to a wall, she had put there.

The image of this collage had burned itself into her brain. Too often, she had stared at every tiny detail. It hadn't changed much in recent years.

But only this morning—she'd gotten up around four o'clock when she'd given up on falling asleep—she had added a few more things.

Dessie walked toward the wall, automatically stepping around the pile of CDs that she knew was in her way. She studied the picture she had printed a few hours ago, one she'd found on the internet. It was an eighteenth-century wood engraving of Scottish women waulking. Dessie had researched this tradition, and there was no doubt that Mrs. MacDonald and her "women's club" had been telling the truth about what they had been doing.

Dessie stuck a thumbtack in the picture's corner, picked up the ball of red wool and the scissors from atop the drink cart and cut a thread. Then she stuck another thumbtack in the corner of a newspaper article that had found a place on the wall close to the picture of the waulking women.

The article was about a regional charity event, and it included a picture of several women. One of them was Mrs. MacDonald. It looked as if she had been turning away when the picture had been taken, and it was a bit blurry. The quality wasn't the best, anyway, black and white and grainy. But it was the only picture of the old lady Dessie had been able to find.

Dessie connected the two pictures with a red thread.

There were numerous red thread connections on the

wall, but they rarely came together to form a web. Sometimes three or four clues crisscrossed, but no more.

Dessie contemplated what to do with the other picture she'd put up earlier. It was a photo of Andie, the one she'd attached to her résumé. It was quite small, and Dessie had had no trouble finding a space for it.

Eventually, Dessie put a thread from Andie to Mrs. MacDonald and another from Andie to the waulking women.

Then she took the photo of Nate she had found on the University of Aberdeen website, where Nate was enrolled, and pinned it in the center of the red triangle.

The triangle—and thus, Nate's photo—now overlapped with a hiking map of the Argyll Forest Park, showing the area Dessie had marked for the inspector. It was a copy of the original she had given to DI Reid, actually.

But Dessie didn't mind. In fact, she thought the overlap added significance to the collage. Maybe the map showed the place where Nate had been killed.

Apparently, the park rangers had not yet found the ritual site…or any crime scene. They hadn't been able to pick up any clue as to what had happened to Nate, other than his phone.

Dessie drew her brows together. Could she trust the information DI Reid gave her? Could she trust the police or anyone from this tight-knit group of locals?

Her eyes fell on the photos of three other women she had found on the internet, printed out, and pinned to the wall. Rosa Simmonds, her daughter Fionna, and Penny Reid. Dessie connected these women to the waulking women with threads, too. The old waulking image represented the strange women's club.

Here, on this part of the wall, she had created a new web, connecting many things and people. But there were only two connections to the rest of the evidence board. From Nate's photo, a very long thread went to Connor's photo, which hung in the middle of the wall. From Connor, the link went back to the Thistle Inn and Mrs. MacDonald.

Then there were Andie and Tara and their connection to Dessie and her B&B. From Dessie's B&B, she needed to add a red line to Mrs. MacDonald as well.

But the picture of Dessie's B&B was also brand new— she had only added it because of her two employees. She hadn't put a picture of herself on the wall at all.

So far, in all her years of investigating Connor's disappearance, she hadn't included herself. After all, she knew she had nothing to do with it.

Now, however, these latest clues were more connected to her than any of the pieces of evidence she had deemed important over the years.

This irked Dessie, and she averted her eyes from the new entangled web of red threats and focused on the older items on the wall, the small details she had contemplated hundreds, perhaps thousands of times.

There was the picture on the summit of Conic Hill, which was part of the West Highland Way. It had been quite a strenuous walk after the first leg through the flat Lowlands, past blooming hedges and a railroad track, through meadows and fields.

But the view was worth it. The Lowlands with their rolling hills and farmlands on one side, on the other the Highland mountains with their rather dramatic, wild landscape. And best of all, the glorious Loch Lomond, divided by the Highland Boundary Fault.

They had taken photos with this stunning backdrop, among others, including the picture of Connor that would end up at the center of the evidence wall. The wind had blown his hair across his forehead—it had grown out a little too long, and he was forever pushing it out of his eyes. He squinted slightly with the sun directly in his face, which made his eyes seem even bluer. His teeth were perfect and his smile irresistible.

THEY WERE ABOUT to continue down the slope toward Balmaha when a couple approached them.

The young man looked at Connor. "You're Andrew, aren't you?" he asked in an American accent.

Connor furrowed his brow, looked away, and shook his head.

The young man didn't seem put off. "Yes, you are. Tom's friend from Hartford, right?"

Connor took Dessie's hand and pulled her away. "Come on, let's go."

Dessie turned her head to glance back at the couple. The young man looked confused and said to his companion, "I could have sworn…"

"Did you know that guy?" she asked Connor, trying to keep up with him.

The young man's question had kicked something loose in her memory, but it slipped away again as she concentrated on keeping her footing.

"He must have mistaken me for someone else," Connor said gruffly.

DESSIE HAD FORGOTTEN about the incident because they'd ended up having a really great time in Balmaha.

Only later, when she'd racked her brain to remember every little thing, every single moment of her time with Connor, did the memory resurface.

She had attempted to track down the couple, called just about every B&B along the West Highland Way in case someone remembered them. But of course, too much time had passed for anyone to recall two typical American hiking tourists whom Dessie could not even describe very well.

Now, going through the incident for the millionth time in her head, Dessie couldn't even conjure up the face of the young man anymore.

She sighed. Dejected, she turned away from the wall and let her gaze travel over the other items in the room. Most of them had come from Connor's old apartment.

Dessie had sold all the furniture except the desk and a dresser, but she'd taken the rest of his possessions with her. This room was like a museum, with artifacts of Connor's life. The fact that everything fit in one room was a testament to the fact that he had led a pretty minimalist existence.

It hadn't seemed like that at all to Dessie all those years ago when she had visited Connor in Edinburgh. In fact, she had been impressed by the stylish furniture and other "grown-up stuff," like a well-stocked liquor cabinet and a pool table.

Connor's apartment had been clean, neat, and modern, wildly different from the student accommodations she knew.

Only later, when she had been faced with the task of disassembling it, had she noticed how few personal belongings Connor had possessed.

She still remembered, as if it were yesterday, when she'd finally had the heart to leave Tarbet and travel to Edinburgh.

She hadn't wanted to leave, felt she needed to be there, in case Connor came back. But the police had asked her about Connor's financial information and family contacts.

Dessie knew that they needed the information to get the investigation under way, so she'd taken the train to Edinburgh.

～

SHE STOOD in front of the door of his apartment with the key she had found in his backpack, her heart pounding.

She half expected to find him there, as if nothing had happened. It was one of the scenarios she had played over and over in her head.

"I'm so sorry, Dessie," he would say with a sheepish smile. "I never imagined myself getting tied to a woman that young, and we barely know each other. It just hit me. I panicked, and I had to get away. It was a mistake, of course. I love you. Will you forgive me?"

And she would. She would forgive him. As long as he was alive and well, that was all that mattered to her.

With shaky fingers, she put the key in the lock and turned it. A soft click. The apartment door swung open. She wasn't greeted by an apologetic Connor, but by stale air and silence.

She walked anxiously from room to room. The apartment looked exactly as she and Connor had left it a few weeks ago. The bed sheets were still rumpled. Two formerly half-empty glasses of red wine on the nightstand now held only a crusty burgundy residue.

Dessie's stomach cramped as she replayed the impromptu marriage proposal in her mind. They had jumped out of bed, thrown on clothes, and quickly packed a bag to head to Gretna Green that same evening.

They'd stayed at a hotel for a couple of days to wait for the registrar to process their marriage notice. "Our pre-honeymoon," Connor called it.

From Gretna Green, they'd traveled directly to Glasgow, and then to Milngavie, the start of the West Highland Way. They'd simply thrown away their travel bag and bought backpacks and camping gear at a store in Milngavie.

Connor had a habit of paying with cash. He always had a thick wad of bills on him. It had sort of suited him, fit this suave, grown-up persona, and Dessie hadn't questioned it.

When the police had asked her about his bank account and his credit cards, she had been ashamed that she, as his wife, did not know about his financial affairs. She'd looked through the things in his backpack and hadn't even found a debit card.

"He must have his cards and his ID on him," she'd told the police.

Inspector Murray thought it was their best bet to track Connor down. Of course, he was of the opinion that Connor had simply run off and would take money out of his account at some point.

Dessie had held on to the hope that the person who had done something to her husband might get greedy and use his credit card. It was unlikely, but still.

In any case, she needed to work with Inspector Murray, and if getting him Connor's financial and personal information would help with the investigation, she'd do it. The sooner the inspector realized Connor wasn't accessing his money, the sooner he'd concede that a third party had to be at fault.

It felt intrusive to search Connor's desk. But she also wanted to feel close to him, and getting his personal information would do that. She had to remind herself that she was Connor's wife—what was his was hers now, too.

She didn't find any bank records, though.

She didn't find any documents at all.

Disconcerted, she turned the entire contents of the apartment upside down.

There was nothing.

No proof of insurance, social security, paid bills.

They'd had to provide a copy of their birth certificates when they got married, so Dessie presumed that he still had that on his person, along with his ID card.

But there was no other such documentation in his apartment.

She couldn't find anything work-related either. No school certificates, employment contracts, letters of reference.

The only thing she could find was a lease for the apartment. The rent included all utilities. According to the address on the lease, the landlady lived in the same building as Connor.

Dessie rang her doorbell, and after an introduction and a lot of hemming and hawing, the old lady admitted, "Mr. McKendrick always paid cash."

No, she hadn't seen any references, an employment contract, or anything like that. She had a feeling about people, and she trusted that. Mr. McKendrick had been "a nice, polite young man." He always offered to help her with her shopping bags.

Perplexed, Dessie returned to Connor's apartment.

She had to admit that all this was a bit strange.

She looked again, this time for any evidence of his work.

Connor had been vague about that, had always said it was too boring, but Dessie was pretty sure that he was self-employed or worked as a freelancer. He didn't seem tied to office hours and could take time off whenever he wanted.

He had mentioned clients, and Dessie was under the impression that his work had to do with finances or business consulting.

But no matter how hard she looked, there were no invoices, tax records, client records, or even handwritten notes that might be related to his work.

It occurred to Dessie that he might be employed by someone after all, or that he rented office space somewhere. That seemed to be the only explanation.

She told herself that all his personal documents had to be in this office, too.

Then there was Connor's laptop. Most likely, he did most of his business electronically. Unfortunately, it was password protected. She tried for a while to guess it but had to give up.

She would have liked to see for herself what was on there, but she felt confident that the police were capable of hacking the computer. Maybe she'd get it back afterward.

Intending to give it to the police, she packed up the laptop and the very few things she'd found in Connor's desk drawer. She returned to Tarbet, planning on packing up the rest of Connor's belongings later.

During the subsequent investigation, the police did find bank accounts in Connor's name, after all. Not in Scotland, but in the US.

Dessie knew Connor had lived with his uncle in the States for a few years, so that made sense.

However, there was no money in those accounts. They had been completely emptied a little over a year before Connor's disappearance.

The police found no proof of employment. There was no evidence that Connor earned his living as a self-employed consultant, either. It seemed that he hadn't been working at all for a couple of years.

It was a mystery where Connor had gotten the cash he

used to pay for everything, but Inspector Murray, of course, suspected criminal activities.

This further supported his assumption that Connor had simply absconded.

Dessie had never bought into that. It just didn't make sense to her. After all, he hadn't had to propose to her. He hadn't had to enter into or continue the relationship with her.

If he wanted to run away, it would been beneficial not to be attached to someone who would come looking for him. Marrying her and running off during the honeymoon —that was a way to attract attention to himself. Connor wasn't stupid. He'd have known that she would move heaven and earth to find him and also involve the police.

In the end, Dessie had kept the laptop. The police might have used it to look for criminal activities, but whatever they would find, it certainly wouldn't point to the third party in Tarbet who had done something to Connor.

Dessie had borrowed money from her father and hired someone to crack the password. Connor hadn't kept any personal documents on his computer, though, and the browser history had been deleted not that long ago. The hacker could only track back a few of the last pages Connor had looked at: information about the West Highland Way.

He had been researching their honeymoon. It was further proof for Dessie that Connor had been excited about their future together and had not planned to run away.

The laptop was still in room number three, in Connor's old desk.

Now, Dessie got it out of the drawer. Ten years ago, it had seemed like state-of-the-art equipment, but now it looked clunky and heavy compared to modern notebooks and tablets.

Dessie hadn't booted up the laptop in a long time—she didn't even know if it was still working. But there had been a time when she had been through everything on there with a fine-toothed comb, again and again.

She'd had periods like that with all the other stuff from Connor's apartment.

How many times had she listened to each of his CDs? Read his books?

Everything had seemed significant, giving her vital clues about every aspect of Connor's life. What if something had a message, and she was not diligent enough, not attentive enough, to decode it?

In the end, it hadn't helped her.

If she was right, then Connor's life—whatever his mysterious past might have been, however he made his living, whatever criminal activities he might have been guilty of—held no clue whatsoever about his disappearance.

All the little details that made up Connor's identity, the details that she had lost herself in for the past ten years, had turned out to be completely irrelevant. The key to the secret of Connor McKendrick's fate lay here in Tarbet.

What had happened to Connor could have happened to anyone—and now it had happened again…to Nate Saunders.

Dessie took one last look at the evidence wall with its newly entangled red web.

If she was right, Connor and Nate had both been ensnared in it.

Her intuition told her these women were guilty. She just knew it, just like she knew Connor had loved her and hadn't just abandoned her.

Dessie left room number three and went to her bedroom where she lay down on her bed, not bothering to get undressed.

She closed her eyes, but she couldn't sleep. One thought went around and around in her head.

Connor is dead, and the witches are to blame.

WHEN DESSIE WOKE UP AGAIN, she realized with a start that it was already dark outside. She had slept the whole day.

She had to admit that it had done her good and that she felt much better. That didn't assuage the feeling of guilt. She had completely neglected her business, hadn't been there to check out current guests or open the door to new ones. Not to mention that no cleaning had been done.

She wouldn't have any help for the next few days either, not until she could find a replacement for Andie. Would she be able to cope?

It felt like it had been days since she'd thrown Andie out, not merely hours. She was overwhelmed at the thought of handling all the chores by herself.

On the other hand, in her rested state, she felt much more confident about the "club" of witches. Grayson was the only one who believed her, but now she was on their trail. Surely it would only be a matter of time until they were caught and brought to justice.

Dessie remembered that she had put Grayson in charge of breakfast many hours ago. She quickly got up—happily noticing that her foot felt much better—and washed her face. Then she went to find Grayson.

He was in the office.

"Hello, sleeping beauty," he greeted her with a smile. "I hope you don't mind, but I went into your room to check on you. I tried to wake you gently, but you were so fast asleep that I couldn't bring myself to do it."

"Sorry, it seems as if I really needed it," Dessie admitted.

"Apologies for rifling through your desk," Grayson said, pointing at the open drawers. "I was looking for stationery to handwrite invoices. I assume you usually use your computer, but it's password protected, and I had to come up with an alternative for the guests who checked out. Rooms one and two."

"Of course, I don't mind. I'm so glad you took care of this," Dessie said with relief. "It's so irresponsible of me to neglect everything and just leave you to your own devices."

"I'm sure that's never happened to you before. And I was here to pick up the slack, like I said I would be," Grayson said in a soft voice.

"I'm really grateful." Dessie looked at the clock on the wall. "I'd better clean the two rooms and change the sheets. There could still be new guests arriving…"

"I've already taken care of it, Dessie. And I checked in new guests for room one. Two young ladies from Norway. Not sure if everything is up to standard, but I did my best, and they haven't complained."

Dessie felt relieved, but also very guilty. "I don't even know how I can make this up to you."

"By finally letting me cook dinner for you," Grayson replied, standing up. "Come on, my famous lasagna is already in the oven."

Dessie had to laugh. "Of course, I can't say no to that. Besides, I'm starving."

That night, Dessie broke her one-glass-of-wine-with-Grayson rule. They didn't mention Nate, Connor, the police investigation, or the witch club.

In Grayson's presence, Dessie managed to forget every-thing that usually weighed on her. She was rested, had enjoyed the lasagna, and felt comfortable. So why shouldn't she let her walls come down, stop hanging on so tightly to a sense of control, just this once?

Grayson had proven that he cared for her, that she could rely on him.

It seemed like Dessie was always fighting someone or something, and she was tired of it.

She wanted to be able to lean on somebody.

And today, she had.

Not just figuratively, either.

When they went to sit on the porch after dinner, a third glass of wine in their hands, she rested her head on his shoulder.

He wrapped his arm around her waist and kissed her softly on the top of her head.

Dessie let it happen.

She felt warm and tingly inside. Guilt was only a tiny dark shadow she pushed far into the recesses of her brain.

They just sat on the swing, arm in arm, silently enjoying the warm summer evening.

Slowly but surely, another feeling washed over Dessie. She didn't recognize it at first, but then knew what it was.

She felt free.

CHAPTER FIFTEEN

ANDIE

"I don't know. Are you sure you want to do that to yourself?" Fionna said skeptically, looking up at the house.

Fionna and Andie stood in front of the stone steps that led through Mrs. MacDonald's front garden to her door.

When they had walked over from Andie's house, the sky had been a bright summer blue dotted with fluffy white clouds. The cloudscape had become denser and now looked gray, which could happen quickly in the Highlands.

One large, almost black cloud hung directly over Mrs. MacDonald's house, like a big bad omen.

Andie wrapped her arms around her body. She was chilly in just a T-shirt. "Yes, come on."

When Fionna hesitated, Andie took her hand and pulled her up the stairs behind her. "Please, Fionna, I can't do this alone, and you promised."

Fionna made a face but followed her reluctantly.

At the front door, Andie pulled the cord that operated the old-fashioned doorbell inside the house. She fought the childish impulse to turn around and run away.

After what felt like an eternity, Mrs. MacDonald

opened the door. She looked more amused than surprised. "Yes?"

"May we come in, please? I'd like to discuss something with you," Andie said, annoyed that her voice was shaking.

Without another word, Mrs. MacDonald turned and went into the house, leaving the door open behind her. Andie took it as an invitation to follow her and nudged Fionna, who stood completely motionless. Fionna finally moved, and Andie closed the door behind them.

They went into the kitchen where Mrs. MacDonald was already preparing tea.

"Sit down," she said without turning around. Again, Andie gave Fionna a nudge, and they both slid onto the old-fashioned corner bench behind the kitchen table.

Mrs. MacDonald shuffled back and forth several times to put two teacups, spoons, milk, sugar, and finally the teapot on the table. The silence was uncomfortable, but Andie forced herself not to blurt out what was on her mind.

Finally, the old woman took a seat on the chair opposite them and pointed to the teapot, encouraging them to help themselves.

The teacups had stains, and there was a smear of red lipstick on Fionna's. Andie could feel Fionna's effort to hold back her repulsion. But they couldn't refuse the tea, and because Andie felt guilty about dragging Fionna into this, she moved the cups close together and poured tea for both of them. Then she took the dirtier cup for herself, hoping her little maneuver had been inconspicuous.

When she looked up, Mrs. MacDonald's penetrating gaze reminded her that nothing escaped that woman. "Milk and sugar?" the old lady asked sweetly.

The milk looked as if it had gone off, and the sugar stuck together in lumps and had little brown spots in it that looked like fly droppings.

"Not for me, thank you," Andie managed to say.

"Me neither," Fionna said quickly.

"Well, then," said Mrs. MacDonald, gesturing at the cups.

Andie suppressed her gag reflex and took a sip of tea. Fionna followed suit. The tea tasted sour, and a tea leaf stuck to Andie's tongue. She swallowed it quickly.

"Now, lassies. What's this about?" Mrs. MacDonald looked directly at Andie.

"I would like to ask permission to let Dessie McKendrick in on our secret."

"Why?" The old woman narrowed her small, dark eyes, which only made her gaze more piercing.

Andie was prepared for the question, though, and had memorized the answer so that, when it came down to it, she wouldn't be at a loss for words. It hadn't helped.

"Fired," she got out. Blushing, she cleared her throat. "Dessie fired me."

"Can you blame her?" asked Mrs. MacDonald, nonplussed. "Your careless actions led her to us. You fed her paranoia."

Andie shook her head. "Not true. I wasn't careless. There was a whole chain of circumstances that led Dessie to us. I had nothing to do with her presence in the woods. She was spying on you, Mrs. M."

She heard Fionna draw in a sharp breath. Suggesting that Mrs. MacDonald herself could be to blame for the whole thing was more than brave. Their leader was known to punish disobedience and disrespect severely. But the old woman only twisted the corners of her mouth into what was probably meant to be a smile.

"And then I happened to stumble upon her, caught her spying on us. I thought she recognized me. She didn't say anything the following day, and I could never get her alone to talk to her about it. Maybe she hadn't seen me, after all?

I thought I'd better not bring it up. Then she followed me to the cabin." Andie took a deep breath. "Do you know what I think, Mrs. M.? That it was no accident that Dessie and I met in the woods. I think she found out about us for a reason. Don't you think it's possible?"

Mrs. MacDonald said nothing, just looked at her.

"In any case, Dessie is now convinced that we're responsible for Nate and Connor's disappearance," Andie continued nervously. "And nothing is going to dissuade her. Nothing but the truth. We should tell her what we are, so she won't suspect us anymore."

"Damage control," Fionna spoke up in a squeaky voice.

"I need to regain her trust. She sacked me, doesn't want to have anything to do with me anymore. That means I can't do my job. Once she knows that we have nothing to do with what happened to her husband, then…"

"But you did have something to do with it," Mrs. MacDonald interrupted her, "at least indirectly."

Andie felt Fionna's eyes on her. She knew she'd have to answer some questions later. She took another sip of the disgusting tea.

"I mean, I have to convince her that I want to help her. How am I supposed to protect her if I'm not allowed near her?"

"Think of something," Mrs. MacDonald suggested. "Maybe Fionna can help you."

Fionna's startled gaze darted to the old woman. "I...um, how?" she stammered.

"Maybe you can do something to use your gift for good, for a change. Take your calling seriously, like Andie here."

Fionna turned crimson. Andie too, but only because she had never received praise from Mrs. MacDonald before.

"That's honorable, Andrea MacLeod," their leader said now. "A lot of young women turn their backs on old values and traditions, and thus their vocation. They move to the city in pursuit of a career, money, or other hedonistic pleasures. You are intelligent enough to have opportunities elsewhere. Nonetheless, you've come home to follow your calling, and you take that seriously. The events of the last few days could have encouraged you to give up. But you came here. I therefore trust your judgment. If you feel you must tell Dessie something, do so. However, choose your words carefully, or she will misunderstand you."

Andie almost forgot to breathe. Fionna also didn't make a peep.

This visit had been an act of sheer desperation, a kind of last-ditch effort to help Dessie. But she hadn't really held a lot of hope that Mrs. MacDonald would agree. Before she could say anything, Mrs. MacDonald continued. "Now, finish your tea."

The young women obeyed, this time without hesitation.

Still, Andie shuddered when she saw the long yellow fingernails on Mrs. MacDonald's hairy hands as the old woman took her teacup. She studied its contents for a moment and then swayed her head back and forth with closed eyes. Her expression gave nothing away when she finally proclaimed, "You know who did it. Trust your intuition."

Then she took Fionna's cup and read her tea leaves. She furrowed her brows and shook her head. "There'll be the devil to pay if ye wilnae quit yer shenanigans."

Mrs. MacDonald's tone was light, but Andie knew Fionna was trying to hide the tears in her eyes as her friend lowered her head and let her red hair fall in front of her face. She took Fionna by the elbow and pulled her off the bench with her. "Let's go," she said.

"Thank you, Mrs. M. You can count on me to do my

best," she said on her way out. She put her arm around Fionna's waist and walked with her down the stairs and then quickly down the street until they made it around the bend. Then she took her friend in her arms, who was crying her eyes out by now.

"I owe you, Fionna, but now please calm down."

"That's easy for you to say," Fionna managed to say between sobs.

"The best thing to do is to follow her instructions," Andie suggested. "It'll all be fine then, I'm sure of it."

"She said I should help you." Fionna broke away from her and wiped the tears and snot from her face.

"Right. Come on, let's go to your house and figure out how to do this."

CHAPTER SIXTEEN

DESSIE

Dessie cursed as she limped toward the office to answer the phone. Her foot was much better, but she wasn't as quick as she would have liked. The door was ajar, and she heard Grayson's voice. "Dessie's B&B."

Relieved that Grayson was there to pick up the slack, she took a moment to catch her breath and smooth her hair before entering.

Dessie felt guilty that Grayson was sitting in her office waiting for new guests. This was his summer vacation, and he probably found the tasks pretty dull. Giving him the password to her computer had been the least thing she could do for him. At least this way he could access the internet, get some of his own work done, maybe.

But a glimpse of the screen revealed playing cards. Oh god, she thought, Grayson had to be bored out of his skull if he had resorted to playing solitaire.

Grayson smiled at her and handed her the phone. "Inspector Reid."

Frowning, Dessie said, "Hello?"

"Mrs. McKendrick? Do you have time to come down

to the station as soon as possible? And bring Nicole with you? I just spoke to her. She doesn't have a car, and I could send someone to pick her up, but I thought you might be interested in what we have to tell her, too...and, well, can you come?" The inspector seemed nervous. So far, she had only ever experienced him calm and confident.

"What's wrong?" she asked. "Did something happen?"

"I'd rather discuss that with you in person, Mrs. McKendrick."

At that moment, Nicole knocked on the door to the office and stuck her head in.

Dessie nodded at her. She knew this had to be about Nate. They must have found something. Maybe his DNA on the spot she had marked on the map, the place where the ritual had taken place.

"Um...yes, of course I'll come. The only thing is…" Dessie pushed a strand of hair behind her ear, looking questioningly in Grayson's direction. "I don't think I can drive yet, with my injured foot." Grayson pointed at himself and gave her a thumbs-up.

Dessie smiled gratefully. "But there is someone who can drive us. I have to lock up the B&B, though. Since there'll be no one here, I have to put a note on the door. Can you tell me approximately how long this will take so I know when we'll be back?"

The inspector was silent for a moment. "I don't think this will take long, Mrs. McKendrick. I'll have one of my constables drive Nicole back if she...uh...if she's going to be here longer."

It sounded like she was correct in her assumption. This would be bad news for Nicole. Dessie tried not to let this realization show in her expression. "Okay," was all she said. "We'll be there soon, Inspector."

After Dessie put a note on the door informing potential

guests that they could not check in until after six p.m., Grayson drove Dessie, Nicole, and Sam to Helensburgh.

On their way into town, Dessie learned Val had moved on.

Sam was very curt when he gave that explanation for his girlfriend's absence, so Dessie left it at that. But she saw in the rearview mirror that Sam took Nicole's hand, and she could guess what had happened.

Arriving at the Helensburgh Police Department, Sam and Nicole rushed through the revolving doors. Grayson offered Dessie his arm, and she took it, but they were still slow to get to the reception area. Nicole was already impatiently biting her nails.

Rosa told them to go straight in.

She seemed so friendly, Dessie thought, as she glanced at her sideways. The woman gave off the aura of a dear old grandmother, but she couldn't be as old as she looked, considering her daughter was not older than twenty-five. It was the gray hair, Dessie decided, styled in that old-fashioned bun, and the reading glasses that sat low on her nose.

Now that Dessie knew Rosa belonged to the witch club, she was sure it was all for show.

They all went through the door into the open-plan office. Dessie was still thinking about Rosa Simmonds when she noticed the young blond man sitting in front of DI Reid's desk with his back to them. Something about him seemed familiar...

DI Reid hastily got up from his chair when he saw them approach and hurried around the desk. The blond man turned his head and stood up as well.

Dessie almost ran into Nicole, who had stopped walking.

"Nate," the young woman breathed, the word barely audible.

Sam led Nicole to the vacated chair in front of

Inspector Reid's desk and helped her sit down before she collapsed. Her face was pale, and her eyes looked feverish as her gaze darted between the inspector and Nate.

With everyone's attention on Nicole, it went unnoticed that Dessie's knees went weak, and she almost collapsed to the floor. Grayson managed to grab her arm in time.

DI Reid rushed over to her. "Mrs. McKendrick, are you okay?" He quickly pulled up another chair.

Dessie carefully lowered herself onto it, and Grayson snapped at the inspector, "What are you trying to do here? Couldn't you have given us a heads-up?"

The inspector looked contrite. "I thought it would be better for Dessie to learn the truth in person instead of over the phone…"

Dessie couldn't say anything. She had the feeling the room was spinning.

Sam said with an uncharacteristically gruff tone of voice, "I think you owe us an explanation, Inspector!"

"As you can all see, Nate is safe and sound." DI Reid hesitated. "I actually thought you'd be over the moon, Nicole. I imagined a more…joyous reaction. I am sorry."

Nicole struggled to speak, but Sam had no such problem. No longer under Val's thumb, he seemed like a changed man. "Where have you been?" he challenged Nate. "Do you know how worried Nicki was about you?"

The handsome young man spoke up for the first time. "I…I just had to get away," he mumbled, looking down at his toes.

"I don't believe this," Sam exploded. "Do you have any idea how many people have been looking for you? All the resources that couldn't be used for other important matters? Damn it, Nate, we thought you were lying dead in the woods somewhere."

Now Nicole started to cry. Sam kneeled in front of her and took her hand. "I'm sorry, Nicki, but it's the truth."

"Everything just got a little too much for me, okay?" Nate defended himself. "The whole vacation, just the four of us, all the time. Man, you guys got on my nerves! And Nicole, you were constantly whining. I couldn't possibly say anything, because you're so sweet and nice, aren't you? So damn delicate. If I so much as hinted that I needed a moment to myself, you started crying." Nate pushed his hand through his thick hair. "I thought this trip would give me time to regroup, to think things through. University sucks. I failed my exams, and when my parents find out, they're going to freak out. I just needed time to think, but the constant nagging and crying…shit, I just couldn't take it anymore."

"You could have at least left us a note," Nicole whispered. "To stop us from worrying."

Nate shrugged helplessly. "I know. That's why I came back."

Inspector Reid cleared his throat. "Nate saw a newspaper article about his disappearance and contacted us."

"I didn't think you guys would get the police involved," Nate said defiantly. "Holy hell, when I saw what a stir you caused, I had to set things right."

"What a stir *we* caused?" Sam cried in disbelief. "You've got to be joking."

Nicole slowly stood up. "I think I want to go now, Sam."

Nate looked at his toes again.

The inspector nodded. "Of course, you can go if you like."

Dessie had been watching the entire scene with the disconcerting feeling that it was some sort of badly acted television show, and she barely registered Nicole and Sam leaving the police station.

"Um, should we leave, too, since they came with us?" Grayson sounded unsure.

137

"Mrs. McKendrick, are you all right?" DI Reid asked with concern. "I know you were convinced that Nate's disappearance had something to do with what happened to your husband, but...well, as you can see, it really was a coincidence that Nate stayed at Mrs. MacDonald's."

Dessie stared at the inspector, then her gaze went to Nate Saunders. *This can't be real*, she thought. *It just can't be.*

"I think I'd better take Dessie home now. The shock clearly has been too much for her." Grayson's tone didn't hide that he blamed the inspector for this.

DI Reid frowned and regarded Dessie with concern. "Yes, I see. But I'd like to talk to Mrs. McKendrick about this some other time. I'll come by the B&B."

"Please call before you do, so I can be there," Grayson said tersely. "Dessie shouldn't be dealing with this on her own."

It barely registered with Dessie that Grayson helped her out of the chair, walked her to the car, and helped her into the passenger seat. Later, she couldn't remember the drive back to Tarbet. All she kept thinking was, "*I was so sure. This can't be.*"

CHAPTER SEVENTEEN

ANDIE

I t was raining cats and dogs, and Andie was glad about it, even though the sound of the windshield wipers was starting to get on her nerves.

But it meant the chances of not being spotted by Grayson were even better. She had parked the car across the street from Dessie's B&B and was waiting for him to exit the building so she could talk to her former boss alone.

Since Grayson and Dessie had followed her to the cottage a few days ago, she feared they would recognize her mother's old red Fiat. So she'd asked in the WhatsApp group, where most of the members of their little club stayed in touch, if anyone could swap cars with her today.

Penny Reid had offered her spacious SUV. Many of the other women weren't a fan of Penny's, but Andie got along well with her. Maybe because she was one of the few women in Tarbet whose husband, boyfriend, brother, or father Penny hadn't had an affair with.

She thought it was nice that Penny had lent her the car she used to transport her wares to market, and which therefore smelled fragrantly of herbs and spices. Fionna had warned her that Penny would call in the favor soon enough, because the woman was not known to do anything out of charity.

Now Andie had been sitting here all morning, watching the door to the B&B. There wasn't a sip of coffee left in her thermos, and her bag of chips was empty. Plus, she really had to pee.

If this wasn't her last resort to speak with Dessie, she would have given up already.

Whenever she had tried to call Dessie over the past few days, it had been Grayson who had picked up the phone. Somehow, Dessie was always indisposed, and even though the American promised to tell Dessie she'd called, Andie never got a call back.

Grayson seemed very comfortable in his role as Dessie's watchdog, Andie thought bitterly. It was possible that Dessie had asked Grayson to fend off her attempts at contacting her. But something told Andie that Grayson had taken it upon himself to shield Dessie.

She hoped that her former boss would agree to at least talk once she stood in front of her.

Andie's patience was rewarded.

Finally, Grayson left the B&B. Andie slid a little deeper into her seat, even though it was unlikely that he would spot her. Aside from using an unfamiliar car, she had taken other measures to be as inconspicuous as possible. Her hair was hidden under a baseball cap, and she had put on her glasses, which she normally only wore when driving.

Grayson got into his rental car and drove away. As soon as he turned the corner, Andie got out and hurried to the front door. The American might only be gone for a few minutes, and she had to make every second count.

She rang the doorbell, but no one answered. It was the time between check-out and check-in, which meant Dessie wasn't expecting any new guests, but Andie was still surprised that she didn't come to the door. Was Dessie not in?

Andie walked around the house to the back yard and peered through the veranda doors. She saw Dessie standing in the kitchen making herself a cup of tea. Andie knocked on the glass pane.

Startled, Dessie looked up. Her eyes widened when she saw Andie. She turned around and stirred her tea.

Andie knocked a second time. Dessie made a hand gesture to indicate that Andie should leave.

Andie knocked again, this time pretty insistently.

Visibly annoyed, Dessie dropped the teaspoon in the sink and came to the door. She opened it a crack.

Up close, Dessie's appearance startled Andie. She had dark circles under her eyes, dry patches of skin on her face, and wrinkles where there had been none just a few days ago. Her hair was greasy and tied up in a loose bun that looked like she had slept on it. "Go away, I don't want to talk to you," Dessie said.

"Please, Dessie, I owe you an explanation. Just give me five minutes. I really need to talk to you."

Dessie was about to close the door again. Andie shouted, "Wait, I want to tell you the truth about us."

Dessie hesitated. "The truth?" She sounded bitter.

Andie nodded.

"Okay. Five minutes." Dessie left the door open, turned away, hobbled to the kitchen counter to get her tea, and sat down at the next table without offering Andie a beverage.

Andie took a seat across from her. "No more crutches?" she asked. Now that she had been given the opportunity to talk, she was unsure and nervous again.

Dessie just raised her eyebrows and took a sip of tea. Okay, no time for small talk.

Andie took a deep breath. "I came to tell you that you were right. We are more than just a knitting and crafting club. We...are a group of women who have a special gift. It's a genetic trait, passed down through the female line, although it may skip one or two generations. My mother, for example, has no..."

She faltered when she saw Dessie's face. Better to keep her explanation short. "Anyway. We've inherited supernatural skills, if you will. Abilities that have always scared people. In the past, our ancestors were shunned or burned at the stake. These days, we would probably not be taken seriously, our practices dismissed as esoteric nonsense. That's why we meet in secret. We're not Satanists or anything like that. And we had nothing to do with Connor's or Nate's disappearance..."

Dessie shook her head in confusion. "What are you talking about, Andie?" She rubbed her face. "Maybe you haven't heard, but Nate showed up again. He just took off, and when he realized the police were looking for him, he contacted Inspector Reid. I saw him the day before yesterday."

"I've heard. That's what I'm trying to tell you. We had nothing to do with Nate, and in fact, it was just a coincidence that he stayed at the Thistle Inn. Still, you were right when you suspected us, and I owe it to you to tell the truth. I...you have to trust me, Dessie."

Dessie sat perfectly still. Her face was a single question mark.

Andie sighed. The conversation wasn't going quite as she had imagined. She tried again, "We're...what did you call us? A witch club. That's pretty accurate. We are witches. A coven. And you did catch us waulking in the cabin, but that's not all there is to it. We perform spells so that the fabric takes on certain properties. It is a very old tradition. Some of us have gifts that allow us to do that. Others are herbal witches or weather witches...Like I said, we all have different talents. We also do ceremonies at certain times of the year, and that's what you witnessed in the woods. It involves sacrificing an animal, you're right. I see why you would find that distressing. But human sacrifice...we don't do that." She hesitated. "It's all actually quite harmless."

"You're telling me you're witches?" Dessie said with dead eyes.

Andie nodded. "I know how it sounds, but…"

"And Mrs. MacDonald, she's, what?" Dessie interrupted her tonelessly. "The witches' superior?"

"Um, yes, something like that. She is the head of the coven. Has been forever. Every one of us has their special gift, but Mrs. MacDonald can do everything. She is very powerful. No one knows how old she really is. But why I'm telling you all this...and normally this is a well-kept secret, but I got special permission from Mrs. M. to let you in on it...I have the ability...um…" Andie broke off because she saw Dessie's formerly pale face getting redder and redder. Her eyes sparkled with emotions Andie couldn't quite identify.

"Have I ever done anything to you, Andie?" Dessie asked through clenched teeth.

"What, uh...no, I…"

"Then why are you doing this? I would never have pegged you for someone who pulls such a nasty prank." Dessie's voice grew louder. "That's the worst, meanest joke anyone has ever played on me. And believe me, I've been through a lot. I'm used to being ridiculed when, after so many years, I still insist that something bad must have happened to my husband. I'm used to people talking about me behind my back. But to make fun of me, right to my face—"

"No, I'm not doing that at all. On the contrary, I—"

Dessie was quivering with anger. She stood up, fists clenched.

"Yes, it must seem hilarious to you when someone spies on you and is convinced that you're a witch and that you're meeting with other witches and that you've sacrificed people to the devil. But let me tell you, it's anything *but* funny when you lose the love of your life and you're so distraught that you believe in all kinds of things. When a whole ten years after this person has disappeared, you still cling to every possibility to blame someone for it, to find out the truth, however ridiculous and nonsensical it might seem. When you lose your mind over the whole thing until you believe in…in witches." Dessie had tears in her eyes.

Andie slowly stood up and raised her hands. "Oh my god, Dessie, no, that's not what is happening. I'm not making fun of you, really!"

"Get out of here, and don't you dare speak to me ever again!" Dessie took a step toward her, and Andie backed away.

"Dessie, I'm completely serious. I do have supernatural abilities…psychic abilities…and I had a vision about you —" Andie, still backing up, ran into the porch door.

Dessie's eyes flashed with anger. "I will not say it again. Get out! Before I do something I'll regret."

Without taking her eyes off Dessie, Andie fumbled for the plaid in her shoulder bag and pulled it out. Frantically, she waved it in front of Dessie. "I brought you something for your protection…"

Dessie stared at Andie and shook her head uncomprehendingly. She backed away a bit, no longer looking upset now, just deflated and sad. "The truth is, I have no strength to fight you, Andie. You won. Please, just go. Please."

Andie reached behind her to open the door.

It was hopeless. Dessie wouldn't believe her. At least not now, not today. Maybe she could try again some other time.

"Okay," she said placatingly. "Okay, I'll go. But what I

said is the truth. I'll leave you this plaid." She carefully placed the red-and-black tartan on the Hollywood swing. "It's made of the fabric we waulked, and we put a spell on it, so it's like a protective shield. Even if you refuse to believe any of the other stuff I've told you…just…just please wear this when you leave the house."

Dessie shut the door and turned around. Andie stared through the glass at Dessie, who slowly walked past her half-empty cup of tea and left the kitchen.

Andie took one last look at the plaid, sighed in resignation, and stepped out from under the porch into the pouring rain.

That could have gone better.

CHAPTER EIGHTEEN

DESSIE

essie shut the door to room number three behind her, leaned against it, and closed her eyes.

She was just so tired, so exhausted. Maybe if she could sleep for a few hours, she could think straight again. But sleep just wouldn't come, no matter how long she tossed and turned in bed. Grayson had given her some pills, but they didn't seem to help either, and she didn't want to take too many.

When she opened her eyes again, she looked at the room and its contents as if she had not seen it countless times before.

She walked over to the stack of books, kneeled in front of it, and picked one up. Jack Kerouac, *On the Road*. She flipped through the volume, even though she knew there were no handwritten annotations on the pages. The book was worn, suggesting that it had been read more than once—but whether by Connor or someone else was, of course, impossible to tell. He might have bought it secondhand.

And even if it had been one of Connor's favorite books, what did that say about him? Every other semi-bookish American man probably owned this classic. It was almost cliché.

Did it say anything about Connor? That he had wanted to break out, be free? In other words, was this book an indication that he had felt too confined by a conventional marriage and had absconded of his own volition?

Dessie had asked herself this question many times over the last ten years, had thumbed through the book, read the odd passage. In fact, she was partly to blame for the condition the book was in. She could no longer be sure what it had looked like ten years ago. It was no longer an artifact of Connor's life, but of her obsession.

That rendered it useless as a clue to Connor's disappearance, but how much of an answer would it have given even ten years ago? It was nothing but her own interpretation, and each book in the pile gave a different, often completely contradictory, clue to Connor's personality, past, and what might have happened to him.

But at least trying to interpret it had given her something to do, had made her feel like she was actively searching for Connor. The objects in this room had always comforted her. In a way, they had been her crutches, helping her hobble from one day to the next, to the imaginary future where she'd get Connor back, or at least find out what had happened to him.

Now Dessie saw the books for what they were. She was suddenly sick of the sight of them. Her gaze went around the room. She was sick of all the objects here.

They couldn't tell her much about Connor, and they certainly didn't hold the key to unlocking the secret of his disappearance. What had she been thinking?

Following an impulse, she went to the small liquor cabinet with the dusty bottles of whisky. A bitter laugh escaped her throat. How could whisky ever have helped her find out anything about Connor other than that he enjoyed drinking whisky? It was ridiculous—*she* had been ridiculous.

She picked up one of the full bottles. A long time ago, she had done some research and discovered that this brand was particularly expensive. She had assumed that Connor had been saving the bottle for a special occasion.

Dessie twisted open the cap and sniffed its contents. The sharp smell of hard liquor made her turn her head. She rubbed the mouth of the bottle with her sleeve and then put it to her lips.

She rarely drank whisky, but she welcomed the burning sensation in her throat and the warmth spreading down to her stomach right now. Dessie looked around the room. She made a decision and toasted it with another swig.

Boxes, she thought. She had to get hold of some boxes to get rid of all this stuff. Too bad she didn't have any right now, because she was itching to get started, now that she had resolved to clear everything out.

But there was something she could do right away, Dessie decided. She set the bottle down, walked over to the evidence wall, and removed the picture of the waulking women. Next, she took down the newspaper article featuring Mrs. MacDonald and the photos of the women from Tarbet.

One by one, the scraps of paper sailed to the floor, and she left them where they fell. She would get a garbage bag later and haul everything off. After removing any reference to her witch club theory, she took a step back. Satisfied, she looked at the empty spaces on the wall that had bothered her before and that she had always longed to fill.

Dessie took another sip from the bottle for extra courage and next tore away the picture of Conic Hill. She deliberately took one item after another from the wall. It felt extraordinarily liberating. She had always hoped that each one of these clues was just the detail that would lead her to the truth.

What she had done, though, was spin a fantasy web. Andie had made Dessie realize this today when she had told her the "truth" about the women's club. You could take any detail of her investigation that in itself held a kernel of truth, connect it haphazardly with other details, and spin a story out of it. A fairy tale. A fairy tale about evil witches who sacrifice people.

By the time Dessie was done, there was almost nothing left on the wall but the red net of threads stretching from tack to tack. The skeleton of her fantasy web, which now looked like a random pattern without reference to the clues that had hung on the wall. In the spot where there had previously been pictures and clues related to her witch club theory, the web was dense and thick, like a malignant tumor.

There was something about it, Dessie thought, drinking another swig of whisky. It was kind of beautiful, like abstract art.

In the middle of the wall, next to Connor's photo, a single document was left. Now that she had removed all the other things, she realized it had been the only real clue she had found in Connor's apartment. The only sign that Connor had existed outside of his apartment, that he had a connection to other people, that something he had told her about his past was factual.

It was a plain white envelope addressed to A. C. McKendrick at Connor's Edinburgh address. The return address was for someone named Charlie Simpson of Connecticut, United States. Scrawled across the envelope in Connor's handwriting: *reply to Uncle Charlie*.

There hadn't been a letter in the envelope, and Dessie hadn't been able to find it in the apartment. Clearly, the envelope had only served as a reminder for Connor.

Dessie knew her husband had been living with his uncle in the US, and she assumed that Charlie Simpson was that uncle. She had passed the information and the Connecticut address on to the police. She had also written to Charlie Simpson, introducing herself as Connor's wife, informing him about her husband's disappearance, and urging him to contact her.

At the time, Dessie had been staying at Tarbet Hotel, and when she ran out of money, she had gotten a job there as a maid. Since she was putting every resource she had into the investigation of Connor's disappearance, she was glad to be able to work there for room and board and thus stay in Tarbet.

There was a computer in the reception area that she had been allowed to use. She remembered like it had been yesterday how giddy she had been to receive the first email from Connor's uncle. She had returned to it, again and again, hoping to get more.

But Charlie Simpson didn't have much to tell her.

Connor hadn't contacted his uncle recently, but they had only barely stayed in touch in the previous years, anyway. According to Inspector Murray, Charlie Simpson had told the police the same thing.

At least Mr. Simpson had asked Dessie to keep him updated with any news about Connor's case, and so they had exchanged the odd email over the years. There had been little correspondence since Dessie had bought the B&B with her inheritance after the death of her father, and she hadn't written to him at all in the last two or three years, since there had been nothing to report.

Dessie took the envelope from the wall and looked at it. She didn't have the energy to go to the office and turn on the computer, so she sat down at Connor's desk. She pulled open a drawer that contained stationery, envelopes, and pens. It was all still in there from when the desk had stood in Connor's apartment.

She hadn't had the heart to throw away even pens and paper and had repeatedly taken them out and looked at them over the years. It struck her now how pointless her actions had been. Why had she kept these things? What could paper and pens tell her about Connor?

It would have been laughable if it wasn't so sad. What a joke she was. She spun around on the swivel chair, reached for the bottle of whisky, and said, "Cheers to that," before taking another big sip.

Dear Mr. Simpson, she wrote. *Sorry for not being in contact recently. I hope you are well. There is nothing new to report about the investigation into Connor's disappearance. I have now decided to part with Connor's possessions. If you, as his only relative, are interested in keeping any of Connor's belongings, I would be happy to send them to you.*

If I don't hear from you, I will donate them to a charity shop. I still have the same email address, so you know how to reach me.

The thought of sending emails back and forth made Dessie feel tired. She'd much rather get this whole thing over and done with as soon as possible.

You can also reach me at the number below.

She wrote her name, phone number, and address underneath, folded the letter, and put it in the envelope. When she copied Charlie Simpson's address from the old envelope, she wondered if it was still current. It probably didn't matter. It was unlikely Connor's uncle would want his old stuff, as he had shown no interest in it over the years.

This letter was more about cementing Dessie's resolve. Besides, it felt like the proper thing to do.

Dessie stood up. Her gaze fell on the curtains that hadn't been opened for a very long time. Well, there was no need to entomb what was left of Connor any longer.

She yanked the curtains open. Light streamed into the room, revealing the dust dancing in the air.

Outside, it was still raining a little, but the sun had broken free of the clouds.

Dessie patted the envelope against her thigh. She was restless—her whole body felt strangely alive. Her fingers were tingling. She felt the powerful urge to get rid of this letter.

She rummaged through the desk drawer until she located stamps. She had to use a few to make up enough postage for a letter to the US—the cost of postage had gone up significantly over the years.

Before she could change her mind, she left the room. Grayson was in the office, but the door was almost closed, and she managed to sneak past him. She really didn't feel like explaining where she was going or what she was doing.

Dessie pulled the front door softly closed behind her and headed for the nearest mailbox.

DESSIE HAD THOUGHT she would feel better after posting the letter.

But on the way back to the B&B, she realized she had overdone it. Her foot hurt, and her steps were dragging. She felt completely exhausted, empty of everything.

She really didn't want to go home. The B&B had always felt like a refuge to her, her command center. But now she realized it was an embodiment of how she had wasted her life. The last ten years had only been about finding out the truth about Connor.

The B&B really only existed around its heart, room number three. Everything around it she had constructed as a home and place of business.

It was a life she had never imagined for herself. Living

in Tarbet, running an inn…this was so far away from what she had dreamed up for her future self.

Now that she had made the decision to dismantle room number three, it became apparent how pointless and empty everything else was.

Her identity revolved around looking for Connor. If she gave that up, everything else fell apart as well. It was too monumental, and she couldn't deal with it.

She was too tired.

Dessie somehow made it to the front door, and when she opened it, Grayson rushed toward her with a frown. "Where have you been, Dessie? I've been so worried about you."

"I was just…" Helplessly, she pointed outside, where the drizzle had turned into pouring rain without her noticing. She couldn't get any more words out. Tears streamed from her eyes.

Grayson reached out to hug her, but stopped when he touched the damp wool of her cardigan. "You're soaking wet! You're going to catch a cold. Come on, let's get you into dry clothes, and I'll make you a mug of hot cocoa."

Dessie nodded through her tears. Grayson led her into the kitchen, settled her in a chair, and helped her out of her wet cardigan. Then he put a pan of milk on the stove. "I'll be right back."

Dessie couldn't tell how long he was gone. Apathetically, she watched the milk begin to boil on the stove, the white liquid bubbling up and over the edge of the pot. The acrid smell of burnt milk wafted over to her, but she couldn't move. She just sat there, frozen.

After what could have been five seconds or five minutes, Grayson rushed into the room. He dropped what he was carrying and ran to the stove, cursing.

Dessie awoke from her stupor and sobbed. "I'm sorry, I was…"

Grayson, who had pulled the pot off the stove and poured the remaining milk into the sink, came over to her. "Shh. It's only milk."

He gently smoothed the damp strands of hair off her face. "It doesn't matter. You're shivering." He picked up towels and a bathrobe from the floor and handed them to her.

Through her daze, she noticed it was the bathrobe from her room. She must have forgotten to lock her door again, she thought fleetingly.

Grayson put the robe around her shoulders and gently toweled her hair. Then he crouched down in front of her, took her hands in his, and gave her an imploring look. "Dessie, you're not well. But I'm here to take care of you. Do you want me to take care of you?"

She was so grateful to Grayson. She didn't know what she would have done if he hadn't been here. If she gave up her search for Connor, she had nothing and no one—apart from Grayson. She nodded vigorously.

"Then let me look after you. You have to trust that what I tell you to do is best for you. Promise me you won't just leave the house without letting me know."

Again, Dessie nodded.

"Good," he said with satisfaction. He straightened and gave Dessie a kiss on the top of her head.

He went to the kitchen, but instead of cleaning up the mess and making another attempt at fixing a cup of cocoa, he just filled a mug with tap water.

Grayson handed her the mug and some pills. They looked like the ones he'd given her previously, but she couldn't be sure. "Here, take these and lie down."

Dessie sighed and swallowed the pills.

She could really, really use some sleep.

CHAPTER NINETEEN

ANDIE

A ndie drove through the rain to bring Penny back her car. She hadn't called her friend to see if she was at home. Andie actually wouldn't mind waiting in the beautiful garden behind the house. She needed time to think, and the garden was just the place for that.

Penny Reid lived between Tarbet and Arrochar. Her large, somewhat rundown cottage came with an immense garden where Penny grew herbs and flowers for her business.

She made soaps, potpourri, lavender sachets and pillows, candles, bath salts and oils, body butter, face creams, and so on, and she peddled her wares at farmers' markets.

At least the products that she had officially on offer. She sold other products under the counter. Opinions in their club differed as to whether that was acceptable. Some looked down at Penny for exploiting her gift for profit. Others applauded the woman for unabashedly using her magical talents and standing by them as much as possible in public, even if it made her unpopular.

Granted, that was the minority. Too many had already experienced the painful side effects of Penny's products and tended to shun her. As a result, Penny had no close female friends.

The fact that Penny was one of the most beautiful women in all of Argyll and Bute—or at least appeared to be—might have had something to do with it too.

Penny had no trouble "befriending" men, however, which was another reason a lot of women hated her.

But Andie didn't have time to sit in Penny's garden contemplating the seemingly hopeless situation with Dessie. When she got to the cottage, she saw her mom's red Fiat in the driveway. She parked the SUV right next to it.

Penny came out to greet her.

Every time Andie regarded the cottage, it struck her how fairy-tale like it seemed. The stones were covered in climbing roses. Blue chalice-shaped flowers framed the front door. The air smelled lovely, as if infused with a sweet but subtle perfume.

Andie knew nothing about gardening. She was in awe of Penny's ability to make everything bloom and grow—even though Andie knew there was more to it than just a green thumb.

"Hello, Andie," Penny greeted her with a pleasant voice. It had stopped raining, and the sun was fighting its way through the clouds—as if the rays were scrambling for a chance to illuminate Penny. They reflected in her golden locks so that Andie was almost blinded by Penny's appearance.

"Wow, dial it back a little," Andie said, shading her eyes with her hand. "It's only me."

"Sorry," Penny said ruefully, and when Andie put her hand down, she wasn't quite as radiant.

"I brought your car back," Andie said. "Thanks again."

"No problem. I didn't even need yours. I didn't have to go anywhere today," Penny replied. "Would you like to stay for a cup of coffee? We can sit on the patio. It has a roof, so we'll stay dry."

Andie had no other plans. After all, her mission had been a bust, and she had no job to go to, so sitting on Penny's patio looking at her beautiful garden sounded good to her. "I'd love to."

"Why don't you walk around the house to the patio while I make us some coffee?" Penny suggested.

Andie knew her way, since she had been in Penny's garden a few times before. Even though Penny was unpopular, her house was a favored meeting place for their group. It was secluded, and there was plenty of space.

Andie sat down in one of the comfortable wicker chairs on Penny's patio and watched the dragonflies buzz across the small garden pond.

Shortly after, Penny joined her with a cafetière of delicious-smelling coffee and two cups. Penny hadn't brought any milk or sugar, but the coffee was so creamy and flavorful that it didn't need it. "Hmmm," Andie approved and took a second sip.

"Can I ask why you wanted to swap cars today?" Penny peered over the rim of her coffee cup with big green eyes.

"Dessie McKendrick. I needed to talk to her, and her boyfriend wouldn't let me see her. They both know my mom's car, so I needed another one for a stakeout. I waited in front of the B&B for Grayson to leave so I could catch Dessie on her own."

Penny nodded, as if it was the most normal thing in the world. "Since you're back early, does that mean you were successful?"

Andie sighed. "Not exactly. But at least I was able to speak to her." She took off her baseball cap and shook out her hair. "Without Grayson."

"Is that the American who stays at the B&B over the summer?" Penny asked with interest.

"Yes, do you know him?"

"Didn't he come to the cabin with her? When she spied on us and called the police?"

Andie nodded. But that still didn't explain how Penny knew he was a summer guest at the B&B.

"He bought something from me," Penny answered Andie's unspoken question.

Astonished, Andie looked at Penny. Grayson didn't strike her as a potpourri kind of guy. "What do you mean? At your stall at a farmers' market, or…"

"No. He came here. Said he heard I specialize in unusual medication. Special potions you can't get anywhere else."

Andie's eyes widened. "What? How did he hear about that?"

Penny shrugged. "I didn't ask him that. I always give a vague answer to those kinds of requests until I find out more about the person."

"And what did he want?" Andie leaned over and set her coffee down on the table. "Probably something to drug Dessie with, right? I knew he couldn't be trusted!"

"Relax," Penny waved it off. "It's not what you think— he hasn't got vile intentions. On the contrary."

"How do you know for sure what his intentions are? What did he buy, exactly?"

"A love potion."

"A love potion?" Andie stared at Penny in disbelief.

Penny nodded. "He told me he has been in love with this woman for years, and he is pretty certain she returns the feeling, but she won't let her guard down. He just needed something to help that along a little."

"And you sold the potion to him?" Andie's voice sounded shrill.

"Why shouldn't I?" Penny replied unapologetically. "That's what I do for a living, and he was a legit customer."

"But you knew that I...that Dessie...and..." Andie was so shocked that she was at a loss for words.

"It was a low-dose potion," Penny tried to reassure her. "There is no way he could harm anyone with it. It wouldn't even work if the woman he gives it to doesn't already have feelings for him. Anyway, he didn't say it was for Dessie. It could have been for anyone, as far as I knew."

"How could you do this, Penny?" Andie's voice rose. "This mission is hard enough as it is!"

"All right, but what does that have to do with Grayson?" Penny interrupted her. She didn't sound defensive, as if she didn't feel sorry at all. "This isn't about him, but about Dessie's husband, right?"

"But I have a bad feeling about this guy, and he's blocking my access to Dessie, making it impossible to regain her trust."

"Maybe you're projecting. It's not Grayson's fault that you lost Dessie's trust. It's your own. His feelings for Dessie are genuine. That's why he bought the potion. Believe me."

"How would you know?" Andie said, taken aback. "If he wants to lower Dessie's defenses, make her fall in love with him, make her trust him, and make her compliant… that's not good. It doesn't mean he's in love with her."

"He must be. He didn't respond to my charm." Penny had the audacity to wink at Andie when she said that.

Andie jumped up. "Penny Reid. You came on to him? I don't believe it!"

"Why shouldn't I? He's incredibly attractive, don't you think?" Penny smiled sweetly at her.

Andie just shook her head, grabbed the car keys Penny had placed on the table, and said in an icy voice, "Thanks for the coffee."

Then she stormed off. Now she could understand why everyone hated Penny.

CHAPTER TWENTY

DESSIE

A soft knock woke Dessie from her slumber.

"Come in," she said.

Grayson poked his head through the door. "Hi. I wanted to see if you were awake. Some chicken broth would do you good. I can bring it to you on a tray."

Dessie sat up and rubbed her eyes. For the first time in days, her head didn't seem foggy. "You know what? I'm much better. I'm going to come to the kitchen."

Grayson's eyebrows drew together in concern. "Are you sure?"

Dessie nodded and swung her feet out of bed. "Yes, I didn't even take my pills this morning, and now I feel much less groggy. I think I've finally gotten over this nasty cold."

The furrow between Grayson's eyes deepened. "You need to take your medication, Dessie. Don't skip it just because you've temporarily improved. You're still weak."

"I'm telling you, I'm feeling better. See?" She went to the dresser to pull out socks, trying hard not to sway. She had been in bed for several days, so it was normal to feel lightheaded, she told herself. Her stomach grumbled loudly. "Do you hear that? I'm so hungry. That's the best proof that I'm on the road to recovery."

Grayson didn't look happy. He was so overprotective, she thought with a smile. He had devoted himself to caring for her the last couple of days and had singlehandedly run the B&B as well.

"I'm going to the kitchen," she said, "and I feel like something a bit heartier than chicken broth, if you don't mind cooking something else." She didn't want to tell Grayson, but his chicken broth had a strange, flowery taste. "Maybe some eggs. Or wait, let me check the freezer. There might be something to heat up. I think I have shepherd's pie in there." Her stomach growled again. "Oh yes, that sounds good."

"Okay," he grumbled.

Dessie went into her adjoining bathroom to wash her face. She was a little startled when she saw her reflection in the mirror. Her cheeks were hollow, and her chin looked pointy. She had dark circles under her eyes, and her hair was very greasy.

Food would have to wait a little longer. She took off her sweatpants, T-shirt, and underwear and gingerly stepped under the shower.

The hot water felt so good on her skin. She shampooed her hair and inhaled the minty smell as she washed it out. Instead of her usual shower gel, she grabbed one with a rose scent that a guest had once given to her and that she rarely used.

After washing it off, she used a fluffy towel to dry herself.

She felt like a new person.

She combed her hair, put tinted moisturizer on her face, and even applied some mascara. Poor Grayson had had to see her looking a mess the last couple of days, the least she could do was make a little effort with her appearance. She dabbed some concealer on the circles under her eyes. Then she put on jeans and a raspberry-colored T-shirt.

Now she was a lot happier with her reflection.

Dessie got butterflies in her stomach when she stepped into the kitchen and saw Grayson's appreciative glance. "You do look much better."

She smiled shyly and sat down. "I hope this isn't too greasy," he said, setting a plate of fried eggs, bacon, baked beans, sausage, and hash browns in front of her. "But it was all I could come up with in a hurry."

"Didn't I say there are meals in the freezer?" Dessie said in surprise. "Shepherd's pie. You could have microwaved it." He shrugged, turned around, and mumbled something. "Never mind," Dessie said with a forced cheer. She didn't want to appear ungrateful. "This looks good, too, and I'm starving,"

Grayson watched her with a half-surprised, half-amused look as she cleared the entire plate. Dessie wiped her mouth with the napkin. "I really needed this, Grayson, thank you," she said seriously. "For everything. I owe you so much. The last few days, weeks, have been terrible. and if you hadn't been here…" She swallowed. "I don't know what I would have done. It's only thanks to you that I'm on the mend."

Grayson stood in front of the porch door and looked out. He didn't turn around, and his voice sounded a little cold as he said, "Well, if you're feeling better, it sounds like you don't need me anymore. I was thinking about booking a flight back home."

It was like he'd dumped a bucket of ice water over her head. "No," she protested. "That's not what I meant. I'm not just talking about you nursing me back to health. I mean, I need you. Here, with me. Whether I'm sick or well."

Dessie was a little surprised at herself. It wasn't like her to just say out loud how she felt, without thinking. She was embarrassed, but then she saw Grayson turning around with a big smile.

"Really?"

Dessie nodded and stood up. She didn't dare meet Grayson's eyes and instead looked outside into the garden. The sun was out. Following an impulse, she opened the door and stepped out onto the patio. She closed her eyes and let the rays shine on her face and warm her skin. It seemed to her as if she hadn't felt the sun for weeks. Months. Years even.

Suddenly, a shadow fell over her, and her whole body prickled with goose bumps. It was Grayson. He put his arms around her. "You're cold. You probably shouldn't go outside yet."

Dessie opened her eyes and met his gaze. Before she could escape from his embrace, he slowly leaned forward. A thousand butterflies fluttered in Dessie's stomach and a shiver ran down her spine. She hadn't kissed a man for ten years, not since Connor. She would have felt far too guilty to enjoy the caresses of another man.

But now there was no guilt—Connor seemed so far away, in the distant past. Dessie existed in the present, and there was only Grayson.

Their lips were only inches apart when the butterflies in her stomach went crazy. Her stomach turned. Dessie pushed Grayson away just in time as everything she had just eaten came back up.

"I knew you shouldn't have eaten such a hearty meal," Grayson said.

Dessie straightened up and covered her mouth with her hand in embarrassment. "Maybe you were right," she said with tears in her eyes. "I should have taken it slower."

"Come on, let's get you back to bed."

Dessie nodded and followed him into the house.

In her bedroom, she climbed under the covers. "Can you bring me a glass of water, please?" she asked Grayson.

He nodded and disappeared for a moment. When he came back, he had the water and the usual pills. "Here, you'd better take two of these."

Dessie put the gel capsules in her mouth but didn't swallow them as she drank a sip of water. After Grayson left the room, she took the capsules out again.

Dessie was never sick, and this long bout of flu was very unusual for her. She wasn't comfortable taking medication over an extended period. After all, she really had felt better, and even though she had overdone it with the greasy fry-up, she didn't feel she needed more drugs. Her stomach, unaccustomed to so much food, had rebelled. That was all. It would settle, and she would be a little more careful about not overdoing it. But she was certain she didn't need to take any more pills.

Still, she didn't want to offend Grayson. It was better not to argue about this, since he had been so good about taking care of her. She didn't want him to think she didn't appreciate it.

Dessie was right. Her stomach soon felt much better, and she read a little until she fell asleep again.

She woke up starving in the middle of the night. She padded to the kitchen in her socks and made herself a plate of cheese-and-ham sandwiches. Dessie took the food back to her room and turned on the TV at low volume, not wanting to disturb the other guests. Munching on her sandwiches, she watched the news with interest. She felt like she had been cut off from the world of the living for far too long—so much had happened in the last few weeks. It felt good to catch up.

She ate slowly and paid attention to her stomach, but it

was fine. In fact, she felt splendid. Dessie watched TV until the early morning hours and then dozed off again.

In the morning, Grayson poked his head in. "I'm going to run some errands," he said. "Do you need anything?"

Just waking up, Dessie sleepily shook her head. "Don't get up," Grayson said. "Let's not repeat yesterday's episode. I won't be long. When I come back, I'll make you a cup of tea and something to eat."

"Okay." Dessie yawned.

She lay there for a moment until she remembered she would like to read the paper. Maybe she could still catch Grayson and ask him to get her one.

Pleased, she noticed she didn't feel lightheaded at all when she got up. She stuck her head through the door to make sure no guests were wandering through the hallway to see her in her PJs and robe.

But it was very quiet. Dessie frowned. Too quiet. She wondered what time it was and went into the kitchen.

There was no one there. The tables weren't set, and the kitchen looked clean and tidy. The clock on the wall said that it was half past eight. Where were all the guests? Had they come and gone, and Grayson had cleaned the kitchen already? That seemed impossible. On the other hand, he wouldn't leave and run errands if everyone hadn't had breakfast yet.

Confused, Dessie went into the office. Through the small window, she saw Grayson's car as he drove away, but she didn't care about the paper anymore. Something felt very wrong.

The board behind the door was full of keys. Only keys for room numbers two and seven were missing. Seven was Grayson's room.

Did that mean they only had room two occupied? Then the clean and empty breakfast room would make

sense, if they only had one or two guests who'd had breakfast early.

But such a low occupancy was completely unusual
during peak season. What had happened?

Grayson had reassured her he was taking care of the
B&B, and now it looked like there were no guests.

Dessie had just turned on the computer to look at
invoices for the last few days and check reservations when
the phone rang.

"Dessie's B&B," she replied absentmindedly.

"Is this Dessie McKendrick?" said a male voice with an
American accent.

"Yes, that's me," she replied automatically. It looked
like they really didn't have any recent bookings, and there
were no new reservations.

"This is Charlie Simpson."

The caller now had Dessie's full attention. "Connor's
uncle?"

"Yes."

"Oh, thank you so much for calling me. I presume that
means you got my letter?" Dessie gnawed on her lower lip.
It seemed like a hundred years had passed since she'd sent
it, and her memory of that day was foggy.

"Yes, I did, and I have to say, I am a little confused."

"Confused?"

"Your letter makes it sound like we have been in
contact before. Like we've been emailing each other?"

"Uh, yes?"

"Mrs. McKendrick, I have never once heard from you
before or wrote to you, for that matter. The police told me
that Andrew got married, but…my nephew and I had had
little contact…I wasn't too surprised that he hadn't told me
about the marriage. I certainly never expected his wife to
reach out to me."

Now it was Dessie who was confused. "Andrew?"

"My nephew. Andrew Connor McKendrick. Oh, yes, he called himself Connor in Scotland. The police told me that at the time."

Now it suddenly became clear to Dessie.

A. C. McKendrick. Andrew. How the hell had she not noticed that at the wedding? She vaguely remembered that Connor had pulled the registrar aside. To tell him to drop his real first name during the ceremony? She certainly hadn't paid any attention to his name on the marriage certificate. She'd been too giddy with happiness.

Connor had taken care of all the formalities and she, in her naivety, hadn't given a single thought to any of that. There had to be a marriage certificate that said Andrew Connor LaFleur née McKendrick, she thought now. Where was it?

Still, the name Andrew must have registered in her subconscious somewhere, which is why she'd placed so much significance on that incident on Conic Hill, when someone had called Connor Andrew.

"Of course," she said, shaking her head. "Andrew Connor...yes. But...I did write you a letter shortly after Connor disappeared. And you responded by email. We then exchanged emails on several occasions. You asked me to keep you updated." How could Connor's uncle not remember that? It had only been two or three years since the last email.

Mr. Simpson was silent for a moment.

"Mrs. McKendrick, I don't know what to tell you, but I have never received a letter from you before. And I certainly haven't emailed you."

CHAPTER TWENTY-ONE

ANDIE

Andie looked around the café. Fisherman's was packed at this hour—there were no spare tables. But she was a good fifteen minutes early to meet up with Fionna. She decided to wait by the entrance.

A blond head turned toward her. Andie recognized the bad dye job before she saw the face. It was Tara.

Of course, she waved Andie over. Not wanting to be rude, Andie walked up to Tara's table and put on a smile. "Hi."

"Hey, you!" replied Tara in her usual exaggerated manner. "I was here with a friend, but they messed up in the kitchen and my order came out really late. My friend had to leave—her lunch break was over. Feel free to sit down."

"That's okay. I'm waiting for Fionna, so…"

"I'll be leaving soon. You can take my table. You'd just have to wait for one, anyway. Come on, I don't bite." Tara grinned.

Andie didn't really have the energy to talk to Tara, but it would look weird if she declined the invitation. She just hoped that Fionna would arrive soon.

Sitting down opposite Tara, she asked, "How are you doing?"

"Great," Tara chirped, spearing pasta onto her fork. "I just looooove working at the Tarbet Hotel. Finally, I have colleagues I can have the odd chat with. And the pay isn't bad either. I have to tell you, the job is a hell of a lot better than my old one at Dessie's B&B."

"Really?" Knowing Tara, Andie thought that the "odd chat" probably meant constant gossiping. She herself wouldn't enjoy that at all. Andie had appreciated that Dessie—and her B&B—were fairly quiet. She'd liked the quaint atmosphere. She realized with sadness that she actually had enjoyed working there.

"Since you've been sacked, shall I let you know if there's a job opening at the hotel? Your parents aren't well off, so you probably need the money, right?"

Tara didn't realize her question was tactless, she was just guileless like that. Still, it irked Andy. Especially because she had to say yes to the offer.

"That would be nice of you. I do really need a job. My hope that Dessie would hire me back is slowly dissipating. I've only managed to talk to her once, and it wasn't a great success. I keep trying, but I just can't get past her guard dog. Grayson." The name slipped out, but now Andie remembered Tara knew Grayson, too. "What was your impression of him?"

Tara bent over her plate, ostensibly to scrape the remains of the pasta dish together with her fork, but Andie suspected she was trying to hide her red face. "Hmm, yes, he made a pretty good impression," she muttered.

"What does that mean? Did you have a lot of contact with him?" Andie asked with suspicion.

"You could say that." Tara couldn't help but grin. "A lot of physical contact," she laughed.

Andie's eyebrows went up. "I don't believe it!"

Tara misunderstood Andie's reaction. "Right? I couldn't believe my luck. I mean, he's like a real man, you know? So attractive and sophisticated and wealthy and well-traveled. A guy like that, he has his pick when it comes to women. And he chose me!" Tara flicked her hair back, glowing with pride.

"Are you trying to tell me you had an affair with him?" Andie squeaked.

"Shh!" Tara looked around, slightly panicked. "Keep it down. It's a secret, okay? You know, like we keep everything secret? That's the reason I thought I could tell you."

"It is not at all like the other secrets we keep," Andie said somewhat sharply.

"Well, not exactly." Tara didn't seem to notice that Andie was not impressed. "But you still can't tell anyone. Dessie can't know about it. Grayson already blackmailed me with this, and I don't want to worry that she might find out. She can't fire me anymore, but she can sure give me a bad reference."

"Wait, what do you mean Grayson blackmailed you?"

"He threatened to get me sacked if I told Dessie he stole a key," Tara waved her hand as she finished the last of her Coke in one big gulp. She burped and stood up. "I've got to be off. Say hi to Fionna from me."

"Wait!" Andie pulled Tara's arm, causing her to plop back down on her seat. "You've got to tell me more about this."

Tara sighed, "All right. So...I can't say he was a sex god, if you know what I mean. A little selfish, to be honest..."

Andie held up her hand. "No, not that. I don't want to know that." She grimaced and shook off the unpleasant mental image. "I want to know about the key. And the blackmail."

"Oh." Tara hesitated. That little nugget of information

had obviously slipped out, and she didn't want to talk about it. "Come on, out with it," Andie urged.

Tara rolled her blue, heavily made-up eyes. "Well…he nicked my keys. After we did it. While I was still enjoying the afterglow, you know what I mean? It wasn't the kind of relationship where we'd cuddle after. It was pretty much in and out." Tara laughed. "Anyway, I didn't realize until I got back home. When I confronted him the next day, he didn't even deny it. Turns out, he was after the key for room number three. Thank god, I didn't have that. I told him only Dessie has a key for that room. I couldn't help but be a little pleased about that, because, well, he tried to take advantage of me, and it didn't work. He got a little angry. Not like, aggressive, just really cold, you know? He warned me not to tell Dessie about the key thing, or else he'd have me sacked for sleeping with a guest."

Andie stared at her. "Did he say why he wanted the key?"

"Oh yeah, I asked him, before he knew I couldn't get the key for the room, when he was still nice to me. He said he didn't mean any harm. He just wanted to know what secrets Dessie kept in that room." Tara shrugged. "That room is weird. I always had the feeling Grayson wanted to hook up with Dessie, and maybe he just wanted to make sure she didn't have any skeletons in her closet. Or in that room."

Andie doubted the explanation was that harmless. She had almost been ready to believe that Grayson's feelings for Dessie were real. She still didn't like the man and found him to be overly controlling, but… He had bought that love potion and turned down Penny Reid.

But then Grayson chose to sleep with someone like Tara and stole keys to the B&B "on a whim." That didn't add up.

Andie's instincts had been telling her that there was something fishy about Grayson DuMont, and it looked like she hadn't been wrong.

That only left the question: What was he up to?

CHAPTER TWENTY-TWO

DESSIE

D essie urged Charlie Simpson to contact DI Reid immediately and report to him what he had just told her.

Then she ended the call and logged into her email account. She located her correspondence with Connor's uncle and forwarded everything to Inspector Reid. She put URGENT in the subject line and wrote: *Charlie Simpson will give you a call. Somebody impersonated him in these emails. I'll be at the station in half an hour to explain. Dessie McKendrick.*

Then she logged out, ran to her room, and grabbed her purse. She locked up the B&B, barely giving a thought to Grayson or any other guests, and set off in her car in the direction of Helensburgh.

The drive gave her time to process, but there were too many thoughts swirling around in her head, and none of them made sense.

Why were there hardly any guests in the B&B? She would have to confront Grayson about that later, however uncomfortable it made her feel. After everything he had done for her the last couple of days, he'd probably think she was ungrateful. But then again, this was her business and her livelihood, and if he couldn't handle looking after the B&B, he should have told her that.

Then there was the even bigger mystery about the Charlie Simpson impersonator. Who had written those emails? How could he have intercepted Dessie's first letter? Mr. Simpson had told her on the phone that he lived alone. There wasn't a wife or children or even a housekeeper who could have taken possession of the letter.

By the time Dessie got to the police station, her head was spinning with possibilities. She was dying to discuss everything with the inspector.

But as she stood in front of the door to the station, she hesitated.

Dessie had given little thought to immediately contacting Inspector Reid. He had seemed the obvious person to pass this new information on to.

Now she had her doubts whether he would even care. He hadn't exactly taken her seriously in the past.

Then again, she had tried to convince him of the theory that a witch club had used Connor as a human sacrifice in a satanic ritual.

Dessie blushed at the thought of how she had gotten all worked up about that.

She couldn't really blame the inspector for keeping a cool head.

Dessie quickly brushed away the memory of Andie mocking her ridiculous theory and making fun of her obsession. She still couldn't fathom how the nice and serious young woman could play such a cruel trick on her.

She tried to reassure herself that there was nothing ridiculous about Charlie's uncle insisting that he'd never contacted her. This was a real inconsistency in the case of Connor's disappearance. Someone had wanted updates on the police investigation directly from Dessie and had gone to some lengths to keep tabs on her and the case.

Dessie pulled herself together, stood up straight, and entered the police station.

Rosa Simmonds smiled at her. "You can go right through, Mrs. McKendrick. DI Reid is expecting you."

Dessie tried to smile back, embarrassed at the thought of what she had accused Rosa of.

She scurried through the door into the open-plan office. Inspector Reid stood up when he saw her.

"Are you feeling better, Mrs. McKendrick?" Genuine concern shone in his eyes. "I tried to reach you on your mobile, but your...friend picked up and said you were sick?"

Dessie frowned. Grayson had taken her phone and answered her call? He hadn't said anything. But that wasn't important now.

"Yes, I'm feeling better, thank you." She took a seat and DI Reid sat back down as well.

"I'm so sorry Nate Saunders's reappearance gave you such a shock. That was insensitive of me. I mean, I under-stand you've waited ten years for new information about your missing husband, and then this terrible coincidence happened... You were so sure that this was a lead. I tried my best not to give you false hope, but..." He broke off. Compassion showed on his face.

Until now, Dessie had always thought of DI Reid as arrogant. She'd thought he'd just dismissed her. In reality, he had simply been worried about her mental state. Rightly so, she now had to concede.

"Uh, yes, I got a little obsessed," she had to admit. "When Nate showed up again, it kind of pulled the rug out from under my feet. It might have been a good thing, you know. Maybe I needed the shock to finally experience... closure." She hadn't put those thoughts into words before, and now that she said it out loud, it sounded harsh. Poor Connor. It felt like she had given up on him, and he didn't deserve that. Dessie swallowed and cleared her throat, but no more words came out.

DI Reid tried to help her out. "I completely understand what you mean. And now, well, there is no closure after all. There's this weird thing with the emails." He lifted a stack of papers—a print-out of the email chain between Dessie and the person who had posed as Charlie Simpson. "I read through them after I talked to Mr. Simpson, and I have to say this has me a little worried." He frowned.

"Well, it's not really a new clue in Connor's case, just an odd thing...and a lot less dramatic than human sacrifice," Dessie tried to lighten the mood with a joke. Her smile might not have been all that convincing, but she still felt immensely relieved that the inspector wasn't dismissing the whole thing. "But it is strange, isn't it?"

"It looks like someone wanted to hear firsthand what's new with the investigation or what you were looking into privately about Connor's disappearance. And you have to wonder who would be interested in that. Interested enough to pretend to be someone else and keep that up for years. Or maybe this person didn't want you to be in touch with Mr. Simpson for some reason."

Dessie nodded. She had arrived at the same conclusions on her way to the police station.

"There are two possibilities," DI Reid continued. "Someone could have gotten hold of your letter by accident. It would be a sick game to play, but in terms of relevance to Connor's case, it would be harmless. What contradicts that theory is that the person continued with this game for years. It doesn't make sense that they would be that invested. If it fell into the hands of a person who was really interested but for some reason wanted to remain anonymous, that is suspicious in itself, but it also could have nothing to do with Connor's disappearance."

DI Reid cleared his throat. "The other possibility is that someone intercepted the letter on purpose."

"I wonder how that could be possible. Mr. Simpson told me he lived alone."

"It could have been a visitor. He may not remember your letter, but it was ten years ago. He might have received it, put it with a stack of mail somewhere in his entrance, kitchen, living room, or wherever, where a visitor could have seen and taken it."

"Then it could have been anyone," Dessie said.

"Well, it had to be someone who thought he'd gain something from emailing you—or from keeping Mr. Simpson from talking to you." DI Reid looked at her searchingly. "There's another possibility. Have you considered that it could have happened on your end? That the letter never even made it across the pond? Did you post it yourself?"

Dessie had to think about that. She had just started working at the Tarbet Hotel. "I put the letter in the outgoing mail at the Tarbet Hotel back then, where I lived and worked as a maid."

"Then I think it's even more likely someone took the letter from that stack," the inspector mused.

Dessie tried to think of the names of her colleagues at the Tarbet Hotel, but there had been quite a few, and it had been almost ten years ago.

The inspector interrupted her thoughts. "If we find out which IP address the emails have been sent from, we might identify the person that way."

"Is that so easy to track? Don't you need, I don't know, a court order or something?"

The inspector seemed to consider how much detail he should go into. "Emails have a source code," he finally said. "We can trace it to locate the IP address of the sender. It's not really a big deal. You can even pay an online service to do that for you."

Dessie's hands tingled with anticipation. If it really was that simple, they could find out soon who had impersonated Charlie Simpson.

DI Reid dampened her enthusiasm. "If this is just a prankster, he might not have done much to conceal his identity. But if the person had any kind of nefarious reasons for making you divulge information about Connor's case, and they knew what they were doing, they might have taken precautions so their emails wouldn't be traced back to them. Also, we can't really narrow down the sender IP to one person, just a place."

Dessie tried not to show her disappointment. Inspector Reid eyed her for a moment. Finally, he said, "I know someone who might be able to help us. I can't promise anything; I'll just say that he's good. It would be a personal favor, not an official line of investigation, you see…" Inspector Reid broke off.

Dessie did not dare say anything. She wanted to refuse out of politeness, because it didn't seem right that DI Reid would go out on a limb for her and possibly get in trouble for it. And exactly why would he cut through bureaucratic tape for her? He didn't seem the type. On the contrary, Dessie would have made a bet that he had climbed the career ladder by following the rules to a tee.

Before she could answer, DI Reid appeared to make his decision without her input and picked up the phone.

He briefly explained the situation to the person on the other end and asked for a personal favor. After hanging up, he forwarded the emails. Then he drummed his fingers on the table and looked at Dessie. "He was confident it wouldn't take long, but you never know with these things."

"Do you want me to wait or…," Dessie said at the

same time the inspector asked, "Do you want to go for a coffee?"

Dessie widened her eyes in surprise, but then stuttered, "Yes…sure."

DI Reid seemed pleased with her answer. He went over to a colleague and talked to him briefly. The colleague looked at Dessie in surprise.

Dessie followed DI Reid out. As they passed the reception desk, the inspector said to Rosa, "I'm going for a quick coffee break."

She, too, seemed surprised.

They went across the street to a popular coffee shop franchise. It was almost empty at this hour of the morning.

DI Reid seemed confused at the many options on the board above the counter and eventually asked for "just a coffee."

He eyed Dessie's mochaccino with hazelnut syrup suspiciously when the barista placed it on the counter. She had to smile. "I gather you don't come here regularly?"

"No," he admitted as he picked up his cup of plain coffee and followed her to an empty table. "We have a coffee maker in the office. I don't really take breaks."

Dessie nodded and took a sip of her mochaccino. That's what she'd thought. Inspector Reid seemed to take his career seriously.

There was a long silence, and Dessie grew uncomfortable. She tried to think of something to say, but she didn't think it was appropriate to talk about Connor's case in public. Small-talk topics just wouldn't come to mind.

The inspector seemed to struggle with the same thing.

Suddenly, it occurred to Dessie that DI Reid might be just the right person to discuss Andie's strange prank with.

"So, Andie came to talk to me a few days ago," Dessie began, stirring the remains of her mochaccino and trying to avoid looking the inspector in the eyes. "I'd let her go the day after I asked you to come to the cabin where the women's group had met. We had a bit of a heated conversation…and I just couldn't have her as an employee after that. Anyway, like I said, she showed up at my place a couple of days ago. It was…bad timing. I wasn't doing well. In hindsight, I really should have apologized to her. After all, it turned out that I had accused her unfairly and then backed her into a corner during our argument. But I wasn't feeling well after the shock of Nate's reappearance and…I guess I hadn't gotten my thoughts in order. She wasn't after an apology, anyway."

Dessie pursed her lips and peeked up at the inspector. She wasn't sure she should continue, but he looked at her with an earnest, genuinely interested expression. She'd already started, so she might as well go on.

Dessie took a deep breath. "She claimed that the story I made up was true. Not the human sacrifice thing, or the connection to Nate and Connor," she said hastily, seeing the inspector's furrowed brow. "But that this women's club isn't concerned with knitting and crafting. At least not primarily. She said that I was right and that it actually is a…witch club. Her words, not mine," she added quickly. "I'm not making this up, I swear. That's what she said. Something about Highland traditions, supernatural gifts, and that I was in danger…" Dessie shook her head. Now that she was telling the inspector about it, what Andie had said made even less sense.

"Believe me, DI Reid, I know I was way off about the satanic ritual crap. I don't believe in witchcraft. Of course not. It had to be a mean joke, right? But why? Andie doesn't strike me as the type to do that. You know her, don't you? What do you think about this? Besides, your sister is part of this group, so maybe you know something that would make sense of what she said?"

Now it was the inspector who looked embarrassed. He

hid his face behind the oversize coffee cup. "I don't have a lot of contact with my sister," he finally said. "We're pretty different."

Dessie nodded and waited for him to continue. Inspector Reid seemed to wrestle with himself. "I like you, Dessie McKendrick," he said finally, to her surprise. "I'd like to be open and honest with you. You could use a friend, and I…" He cleared his throat and blushed again. "I can't talk to you about this as DI Reid, but privately…" He put down his coffee cup and held out his hand to her. "Well, I'm Declan."

This was so unexpected that Dessie hesitated for a moment until she saw the disappointment in his eyes. "Dessie," she said unnecessarily, and had to bite back a smile as she shook his hand.

"Well, Dessie," Declan sighed. "It's not a particularly well-guarded secret around here that my sister and her friends are a little…unorthodox. I don't really want to know too much about their activities, to be honest. One thing to bear in mind is that Highlanders are a wee bit more superstitious than the rest of the Scots, particularly city dwellers."

Dessie wanted to interject, but Declan beat her to it by quickly saying, "Look, the fact is that my sister has an extraordinary talent for growing plants. She is very knowledgeable about herbs and such. She has helped many people in Tarbet and the surrounding area. So they look the other way when something a little more unusual happens in her garden. The same goes for some of the other ladies in that little club of theirs. I hadn't known Andie was one of them, no. But she does strike me as a sensible girl, and I can't imagine she was playing a cruel joke on you. Maybe you misunderstood her. Is it possible you misinterpreted something because you weren't feeling well? You told me how upset you were at the time, and you were actually sick…"

Dessie nodded slowly. "That's true. But she did say witches. I didn't misinterpret that. That was the word she used."

"Maybe they are witches." Declan Reid shrugged help-lessly. "My sister may be an herb witch. That fits. They used to say that about my mother, too." At her questioning look, he stiffened a bit. "She died when I was little," he explained. "I'm just saying, the word witch is loaded with associations of, I don't know, broomsticks and pointy hats, and frog legs and eyes of newt in slimy green potions bubbling in cauldrons. But what this women's club is doing could be something totally harmless. I think they're just keeping up old Highland traditions and, sure, they might seem witchy to modern folk."

"Hmmm." Dessie decided to speak to Andie again. Whatever she had meant by her confusing admission that the knitting and crafting club was, in fact, a witch club, DI Reid seemed to think she had meant no harm.

No, not DI Reid, Dessie thought. Declan. The corners of her mouth drew up.

They finished their coffee in silence, but this time it wasn't awkward. On the contrary, Dessie realized that she felt comfortable in Declan's presence, even when they weren't talking.

As they got up to leave, Declan said to her, "Wait a second. Before we return to the station and I have to step back into my role as Detective Inspector, I want to ask you something. I feel much more comfortable asking you as a friend."

Dessie sat down again, unsure whether she should be excited or nervous.

Declan took a seat again, too, and looked at her in earnest. Dessie's stomach flipped.

"Have you considered that it could be Connor who wrote those emails? After all, if Inspector Murray was right and there was no crime, if Connor just took off, who would have a greater interest in knowing how the investigation is going than Connor himself?"

Dessie was taken aback. That was not at all the question she had expected.

"No," she finally managed to get out. "No, that possibility didn't occur to me at all."

"How do you feel about that? Could you deal with that? If he was still alive?" Genuine concern shone in Declan's warm brown eyes.

She thought about it for a moment. It seemed to her that if the emails had come from Connor, she would have known somehow. That she would have recognized his words. Then she shrugged. "A week ago, I couldn't have handled it, to be very honest. But now…" She sighed and shook her head. "I just don't know."

"We really should hope that it is Connor."

Dessie's eyes widened in surprise. "Yes, of course we should. There's nothing I wish more than to be proven wrong."

"Yes, of course, but also…" Declan brushed a hand through his hair. "If Inspector Murray was wrong, and you were right…if Connor was a victim of a crime…who would be interested in finding out what you and the police have turned up in the investigation? The perpetrator. In that case, the emails might have come from Connor's killer."

Dessie suddenly became very cold.

Her gut told her that Declan was right.

She knew Connor was no longer alive.

It was completely irrational, but at that moment the superstitious Highlanders didn't seem ridiculous to her at all. At that moment, gut feelings and visions appeared as real as gravity and electricity.

At that moment, she was even ready to believe that Andie MacLeod was a witch.

~

WHEN DESSIE and DI Reid got back to the station, there was no news about the IP address yet.

Declan promised to call as soon as he heard anything, and Dessie drove back to Tarbet.

She had just parked her car in front of the B&B when someone knocked loudly on her window. Dessie flinched. It was Grayson, and he looked upset.

Frowning, she opened the door. He took her by the arm to help her out of the car, but his grip was a little too tight. "It's okay, I can walk by myself."

"Where have you been?" Grayson snapped at her as he dragged her into the house.

"Grayson, what's going on with you?" she cried, escaping his grip.

He shut the door and locked it. Without another word, he rushed past her, farther down the corridor.

Dessie followed him, completely confused. "Why are you so upset?"

"You should be in bed. You promised me you wouldn't leave the house without telling me!" He had turned around, but the corridor was dark, and his face was in a shadow. She couldn't really read his expression; she only knew he sounded very hurt.

"I…" She didn't know how to respond. "I'm feeling much better. Seems like I'm over this flu. I don't have to be in bed anymore."

Grayson remained silent. Dessie moved toward him.

Now she could see Grayson's face. It was contorted with anger into an ugly grimace, but his expression smoothed within seconds. Maybe the shadows had played tricks on her.

"I was so worried," he said. "I just went on a few errands, and you were sick in bed, and then I come back, and you're just gone."

"You could have called me," Dessie said, a little relieved.

He had been worried about her. Of course. It was panic, not anger, she had seen in his face. She just wasn't used to letting someone know where she went. She walked up to Grayson and took him in her arms.

He stiffened, but relaxed as she stroked his back. "I'm sorry," she said. "I didn't think of that."

"Your phone is in the office," he said a little defiantly. Maybe he was embarrassed that he had shown such concern. "I couldn't get a hold of you."

When he mentioned the office, Dessie remembered the few reservations and the unoccupied rooms. She broke away from him. "Grayson, what's going on with the B&B? Why is it so empty? We should have plenty of guests in high season."

He gave her a bright smile. "Oh yes, that reminds me. I have a surprise for you. Why don't you go on into the kitchen and I'll be right there." Grayson turned away from her and walked down the hall toward his room.

Puzzled, Dessie looked at his door for a moment before moving down the corridor. She pushed open the door to room number one. It was unoccupied. As were all the other rooms she checked on her way to the kitchen. The guests from room number two had apparently checked out, too.

The B&B was completely deserted. An uneasy feeling crept over Dessie. She went back to the office to grab her phone. The inspector hadn't called yet, but it showed ten missed calls from Grayson.

He hadn't come back out of his room yet, so Dessie went into the kitchen. There, she paused, indecisively. Before she could come to any conclusions about the situation, Grayson rushed in carrying his laptop.

"Grayson…" she began, but he came to the closest table and all but pushed her into a chair. Then he put the laptop in front of her, tapping a key to make the screen come alive. Dessie looked at a photo of palm trees, turquoise water, and a white beach. She looked up at Grayson questioningly.

"When was the last time you went on vacation, Dessie?" She furrowed her brows, but before she could answer, he continued. "I bet you haven't been away once in the last ten years, am I right?" He sat down opposite her at the table and turned the laptop around. "Dessie, after all you've been through, you deserve to make your own well-being a priority and get pampered. I've booked us a three-week vacation at a spa hotel in the Bahamas. We're leaving the day after tomorrow."

He looked at her expectantly, but Dessie couldn't get a word out. She was torn. Three weeks in the Bahamas sounded great, and it was wonderful of Grayson to think of this. At the same time, she felt completely caught off guard, and she didn't like that. Finally, she managed to get out, "That's so sweet of you, and I'm so grateful. But I can't be away from the B&B for that long. It is my busiest time. And besides…"

"I've taken care of that! I've canceled all the reservations and haven't taken new ones, so you can close the B&B for the next couple of weeks. Believe me, Dessie, this break will do you good. It's just what you need."

Now it all made sense to Dessie. She put her head in her hands. "That's why there aren't any guests! You turned them away? And canceled all the reservations? Oh, god, Grayson! I depend on the tourists in the summer. It's when I make most of my money. I need to be at maximum capacity during this time to keep the business afloat throughout the year."

It horrified Dessie that Grayson had done such a thing without asking her, but she felt relieved that there was an explanation for his behavior.

"What you need is a break, a vacation, time to yourself." The corners of Grayson's mouth drooped.

Dessie put her hand on his arm. "Believe me, I would love to. I'm grateful to you for arranging this for me, for even thinking about this. And it would be a dream. I couldn't imagine anything better than lying on the beach with you and enjoying the sun. But I can't leave here. I can't afford to do that."

"Of course you can. It's not like you depend on the B&B income for money. And when you get back, you'll have bookings again in no time. There are always tourists in Tarbet…"

"What makes you think I'm not financially dependent on the B&B?" Dessie interrupted him, completely surprised that he made this assumption. "What do you think I live on?"

Now it was Grayson who looked puzzled. "I thought...you had an inheritance."

Dessie shook her head. "When my father died, I inherited his estate. It was basically his house, and I sold that. I used the money to buy this B&B. There wasn't much left after that. What on earth gave you the impression that I'm independently wealthy?"

Grayson gave her a strange look that she didn't know how to interpret. He was probably just disappointed. Or did he think she was ungrateful?

"I'd love to go some other time, though. Maybe later in

the year when it's less busy here. It's not a good time right now, for so many reasons…" She paused. Grayson didn't know about Charlie Simpson and the emails yet. "I just came back from talking with Inspector Reid. I left in such a hurry, without taking my phone or leaving you a message, because suddenly there's a new lead in Connor's case."

Grayson's right eyelid twitched, but otherwise, his expression stayed the same. "Really?"

Dessie told Grayson what had happened. "So maybe they can find out this imposter's IP address and track him down. The inspector might call with news any minute now. Imagine, after all these years, I was ready to give up—and now this happens. There's still a chance that the emails were just a tasteless joke and the person had nothing to do with Connor's disappearance. But they might lead to the answer I've been looking for."

"That's wonderful news, Dessie," Grayson said quietly. "Maybe this will really give you closure, and our vacation will have even more meaning. You're right, we should just postpone it. Let me take care of it right now." He stood up and was about to take his laptop.

Dessie grabbed it. "No, wait. I want to look at pictures of the spa resort. You've gone to so much trouble. And I could really use a distraction and something to look forward to."

He hesitated, still pulling at his laptop. Again, his expression was unreadable.

Dessie had to swallow. "I'm sorry I dismissed your idea at first. You took me by surprise, that's all. Now I really want to go."

He nodded slowly. "Okay. Wait a second." Grayson typed something in and called up a website. Then he turned the laptop around. "This is the resort. Just click through the gallery. I'll use my phone to find the number and call them up to move the reservation to October. How does that sound?"

Dessie smiled. "Perfect. Thank you."

"Okay, I'll be right back."

Dessie turned her attention to the stunning photos of the spa resort. It really looked like paradise.

A few minutes later, Dessie's phone rang. It was DI Reid. Her fingers trembled as she pressed the button to answer the call. "Yes?"

"Dessie? It's Declan. Are you at home?" The inspector sounded agitated.

"Um, yes. Have you heard anything about the Charlie Simpson emails yet?"

"Yes. Dessie, listen carefully! The last couple of emails. They were sent from your house!"

CHAPTER TWENTY-THREE

ANDIE

A ndie stomped up the stairs to Fionna's room.
Fionna even had a door phone with a buzzer in her room, so she didn't have to come down to let someone in.

Her friend really took laziness to a new level, Andie thought, disgruntled. Then she immediately felt guilty and reminded herself not to take her bad mood out on Fionna. That would be grossly unfair. After all, Fionna had called Andie with an idea of how to help her.

Andie's resolve was put to the test when she saw the mess in Fionna's room. Clothes were scattered everywhere. She counted at least six empty mugs placed around the room. The bed was unmade, and there was a pile of books on the nightstand that reminded her of a game of Jenga. Hopefully, Fionna wouldn't one day accidentally knock over the stack in her sleep and get buried under it.

Andie swept newspapers, candy bar wrappers, socks, and sweaters off the couch before she sat down. She slid down carefully so she wouldn't hit her head on the low slanted ceiling above the couch.

She was about to tell Fionna off for eating too much

chocolate when she felt a candy bar under her left thigh. She pulled it out. It was unopened. Chocolate-covered peanuts and caramel. She could use one of those right now.

"Hey!" Fionna protested from her desk chair, peering out from behind another pile of books. "That belongs to me. I've been looking for that one."

"Finders keepers," Andie mumbled with her mouth full.

"How about a hello, how are you doing, before you eat my snack?" Fionna said. "What's going on with you?"

Andie waved it off. It was impossible to talk around the glob of sticky caramel-peanut mixture in her mouth, anyway. She didn't even want to get into her last failed attempt to talk to Dessie. Again, it had been Grayson to open the door at the B&B. And again, he'd told her that Dessie wasn't available.

Andie hadn't seen her car parked in front of the B&B, so maybe the American had been telling the truth this time.

There wasn't much chance that Dessie would talk to her, anyway, even if she would have been in. Andie had left her several voice messages over the past few days, and Dessie hadn't returned one.

"Didn't get past the guard dog again, huh?" Fionna asked, crinkling her freckle-covered nose. Andie rolled her eyes and nodded.

"Dessie doesn't seem to want to listen to your warnings," Fionna continued. "So I figured we need to find a way to protect her, even if she doesn't cooperate. The plaid was a good idea, but if she doesn't believe you, she might not wear it. And what if she's in danger in her own house? Or she leaves the house when it's warm out, like today? Then she won't need a wool plaid. At first, I thought maybe I could enchant some other object to attach to her person. A pin or something. But Dessie doesn't even let you close enough to her for you to pin it on her. Even if you did manage to get it on her person somehow, she might notice and remove it, or change clothes…and we would have the same problem as with the plaid. No, if she isn't willing to voluntarily keep an object enchanted with a protection spell on her person, we can't force it on her. My magic is useless, in this case. We need to ask someone else for help."

Fionna's cheeks flushed with excitement. Andie was touched that her friend had gone to such much trouble to help her. Whatever her faults, Fionna's heart was in the right place. "And who did you have in mind?" She crumpled the empty chocolate bar wrapper in one hand and looked around for a trash can. Finding none, she simply dropped it next to the couch, where it was in good company.

"Penny Reid."

"Penny? Ugh!" She did nothing to hide the contempt in her voice.

"Huh? Since when do you have something against her?" Fionna asked, surprised. "You borrowed her car just the other day, didn't you?"

Andie told Fionna about her conversation with Penny and that the herb witch had sold Grayson a love potion and had tried to seduce him.

"Hmm," Fionna said. "Still, she's our best bet. I found a protection spell in one of my books. Penny will know how to do it, and she'll have all the ingredients we need."

"I don't know, Fionna." Andie wasn't sure she could trust Penny.

"Well, there's only one other person who could help us with the protection spell, and if you want to go and consult her, I'm sorry to say, you're on your own." Fionna shuddered. "I still have nightmares from the last visit."

Andie crinkled her nose. "You mean Mrs. M." After a

brief pause, she said, "You're right. Mrs. MacDonald will know what to do. But we already went out on a limb with her when we asked for permission to tell Dessie our secret. That failed big time, and I don't dare ask her for anything again so soon. Penny may be a cold and selfish witch, but asking her is still better than approaching Mrs. M."

Fionna seemed relieved. She got up from her desk chair. "Let's go downstairs. I'll show you what I found."

Andie followed her friend down the two flights of stairs into the basement. It was a cavernous room, and apart from the old-fashioned fireplace and a freezer on one wall, it was filled with a maze of bookshelves.

It was too dim to see much—there was no other light source but a brass chandelier with faulty electric candles hanging from the ceiling.

It didn't seem to be a problem for Fionna, as she knew her way around blindly here, in her own realm. Considering what Fionna's room looked like, it was surprising how neat and well organized everything was.

"All right, where did I put the book on protection spells? Oh, yes..." Fionna confidently approached a shelf in a dark corner.

Andie's gaze wandered along the ancient-looking leather-bound tomes. Some of these had to be worth a lot of money, even though they didn't look it. Fionna collected rare books and sold them to other collectors via her website. It wasn't an official business; Revenue Scotland certainly didn't know about it.

It could very well be that Fionna made some of these books even more rare and valuable with her special gift. Her friend didn't talk about how she was able to enchant books or for what purpose, but Andie knew Fionna wasn't just in it for the profit. She really didn't care about money, so she had to get some other benefit out of it.

Fionna loved books—maybe that's all there was to it.

Andie could sense that some of the tomes in the basement were enchanted. There was a buzzing in the air, kind of like an electric current, that caused the hairs on her arms to stand up.

She had asked Fionna before what the big fireplace was used for, but she hadn't really gotten an answer. It was probably just left over from whatever Rosa's mother, Fionna's grandmother, had practiced down here. Matilda Simmonds had been a very powerful witch. Fionna didn't like to talk about her or about what had gone on in this basement in the past.

Fionna had apparently found what she was looking for, because she returned to Andie with a thick, leather-bound volume. A satisfied smile spread across her face. She was about to open the book, but Andie said, "Let's go back upstairs. It's chilly down here." She wrapped her arms around her body.

"I hadn't noticed," Fionna said. "But all right. Let's go upstairs. We'll study the protection spell I have in mind, and then we can pay Penny a visit. Even if you guys had a fight the last time you spoke, she's obligated to help us if we ask her."

CHAPTER TWENTY-FOUR

DESSIE

The inspector's words sent an icy chill down Dessie's spine. The emails had been written here, in her B&B? How could that be? Who could that be?

After Declan assured her he was on his way to see her and discuss the matter further, she stammered a thank you and simply lowered the phone.

Her hands felt numb. A thousand thoughts buzzed around in her head without connecting to anything that made sense. She forced herself to push all of them back and think logically.

Nobody had access to her computer except herself. But of course, she had given out the password occasionally, asking her employees to take tasks over from her.

Tara had worked here for the last three years, Andie this summer...and they were both part of this secret organization, whatever it was supposed to be.

But wait...The emails had stopped two, no, three years ago. That was before Tara had started working here. There had been different summer help over the years, but there wasn't one employee who would have had access to her computer consistently.

The computer in her office wasn't the only option. Guests brought laptops and phones, of course. It was possible someone had used a phone to write these emails, right? Would they have an IP address? She'd have to ask the inspector.

But then a thought occurred to Dessie. She did have repeat guests, though not consistently, so they could have been responsible for sending these emails from the B&B.

But there was only one permanent guest who had been here every summer for years.

Grayson.

Slowly, she stood up. Her knees trembled as she walked toward the kitchen door. Carefully, she pushed it open. It was eerily quiet in the hallway.

Grayson must have gone to his room to make the call to the spa resort.

Dessie didn't dare breathe as she crept toward the door to room number seven.

When she paused in front of it to listen, she didn't hear anything but her own loudly beating heart.

Slowly, ever so slowly, she pushed against the door.

It wasn't locked.

Dessie peeked through the gap. She couldn't see Grayson, and she definitely couldn't hear his voice. Swallowing hard, she opened the door even further.

There was no sign of Grayson. She slipped in, tiptoeing to the bathroom. It was dark and empty.

Dessie turned around and looked at the room more closely. The closet doors were open; hangers had dropped to the floor.

There were still some items in the closet, but it looked as if Grayson had grabbed everything in a hurry. She couldn't spot a suitcase, either.

A dark sense of foreboding crept over Dessie, and she stumbled to the window, hastily pulling aside the curtains. The space where Grayson's car had stood was empty.

Dessie raced through the B&B, opened doors everywhere, searching every room and bathroom.

When she was satisfied that she was completely alone in the house, she locked the front door from the inside. All the while, she was trying to come to terms with the fact that, while she had been looking at the pictures of the resort in the Bahamas and talking to Declan on the phone, Grayson must have quickly packed up his things and left.

Dessie remembered his facial expression when she had told him she expected a call from DI Reid, possibly with information about the person who had written the emails.

She just hadn't wanted to see it.

But it was clear to her now that Grayson had been trying to hide his guilt and anger at being found out.

Well, his sudden exit was enough to prove that she was right in her suspicion that Grayson had been the Charlie Simpson imposter.

Wait, she thought. There might be actual proof.

She ran into the kitchen. Grayson's laptop was still on the table where she'd left it. He surely knew that it could contain damning evidence, but he must have decided to cut his losses.

Dessie sat down and closed the browser showing the spa resort photos with a shaky hand.

Grayson's email account was password protected.

Without thinking too much, Dessie typed in ConnorM-cKendrick, but it was the wrong password. She tried a few other combinations of Connor's name without success. Her fingers trembled as she entered DessieMcKendrick and then DesdemonaMcKendrick, both of which turned out to be wrong.

Heat rose to her cheeks. Of course, he hadn't used her

name. Grayson hadn't really cared about her. He had only faked his friendship to...what? To get information? After all, he'd already accomplished that by exchanging emails. Why had he bothered to come here every summer, to befriend her, to win her heart?

Dessie took a deep breath. She closed her eyes and pushed all thoughts of Grayson's deceit aside. She had to keep a cool head. Suddenly, the right password came to her.

AndrewMcKendrick.

She typed it in, clicked enter, and the account opened.

First, she checked the sender's address. It wasn't ChSimpsonConnect@hotmail.com, she noticed, slightly disappointed. But that didn't necessarily mean anything. Grayson could have just opened the fake Charlie Simpson account for the specific purpose of duping her. This clearly was his own account, which he used for business and personal emails, she discovered, when she scanned the most recent mail.

On a whim, she searched all folders for McKendrick.

Dessie nearly fell off her chair when the search turned up her entire conversation with "Charlie Simpson." Grayson had set up automatic forwarding of her responses to his inquiries.

She leaned back and exhaled slowly. Here was proof.

Grayson was responsible for the emails, had almost certainly written them himself.

Dessie could hardly believe it.

Thunderstruck, she sat there staring at the screen.

It took her a while to notice that there was another email containing the search term McKendrick that had nothing to do with the imposter email chain. Anxiously, she opened it.

Hey, are you still looking for Andrew? A buddy of mine swears he saw him just yesterday. You won't believe where—in Scotland! It prob-

ably wasn't him. My buddy is on a hiking holiday and claims he saw him on some mountain. Conic Hill. Thought I'd let you know. Richard.

Dessie felt faint. She grabbed the edge of the table, reading the brief message again and again.

The couple on the top of Conic Hill had recognized Connor as Andrew McKendrick. The real Charlie Simpson had called him Andrew, too.

Why had her husband not told her he had gone by another first name most of his life? And why had he brushed off Richard's friend, pretending that he wasn't Andrew?

Dessie didn't have the answers, but the emails told her that Grayson had been trying to find Connor, and Richard's email had put him on the right trail…only a day before Connor disappeared.

The doorbell rang, and Dessie's heart skipped a beat. Panic-stricken, she jumped up.

Then it occurred to her that Grayson wouldn't ring the bell. It had to be Declan.

"You're white as a sheet," DI Reid greeted her with a frown when she opened the door. "Is everything okay?"

"I know who wrote the emails," she replied tonelessly.

She asked Declan to follow her to the kitchen, where she showed him what she had found on Grayson's laptop.

"And you didn't suspect him at all, all those years?" Declan asked.

"I guess he's an excellent actor," Dessie said bitterly.

Declan eyed her. "I had the impression that he was more than a guest…that he was a friend…maybe more?"

"At least I didn't make it easy for him," Dessie said. "Until this summer, I hadn't let him into my heart. But after everything that's happened in the last few weeks, I was just…"

"Vulnerable," Declan finished her sentence.

"I was going to say I was an easy target for a con artist," she said dryly.

"Dessie, I hope you don't let this experience harden your heart again. That would be a real shame." Declan clearly was embarrassed to have spoken so frankly, because he stared at a spot on the tablecloth instead of looking her in the eye.

Dessie sighed. "I thought he was my friend," she said quietly. "And because I had only one priority in my life for a decade, which was to find out what happened to Connor, he was pretty much my only friend. Turns out, he was just using me."

Declan reached out, but only nudged her hand. "That's not true. I'm your friend, too. I thought you and I agreed on that at the café." He smiled wryly, and Dessie couldn't help but smile back.

The inspector cleared his throat. "Hmm. Do you have any idea why Grayson put so much effort into this all these years? Writing the emails is one thing, but coming here every summer… That's far too involved for this to be a sick prank."

Dessie shook her head. She told Declan how Grayson had taken care of her over the past few days. "I thought he was devoted to me, but now I know he was trying to control me. He made sure I was sick in bed so that he could snoop around. I gave him the password to my computer, left him in charge of the B&B. He had to be looking for something specific. I have no clue what that could be. It seems like hearing updates from me about Connor's case wasn't enough. Did he perhaps think I knew something about Connor's disappearance that I wasn't admitting?" Perplexed, she looked at the inspector.

He shrugged his shoulders. "Whatever it was, he doesn't seem to have found it, or he wouldn't have stayed here playing his role until today. He only left so abruptly when it seemed we were hot on his trail."

Dessie frowned. "What I still don't get is how Grayson could have gotten hold of my first letter to Charlie Simpson. Was he here in Tarbet when I mailed it? At the Tarbet Hotel? I almost can't imagine that."

"Maybe the letter was intercepted in the US after all. Grayson is an American," Declan mused. "Why don't we ask Mr. Simpson? It could be that he knows Grayson. What else does he have on his laptop? Are there any photos of him? Have you looked through all his emails yet?"

Dessie shook her head. "No, I've only had time to find what I told you about."

The inspector looked at his watch. "Well, it's the middle of the night in Connecticut, anyway. Let's see if we can find anything here before we ring Simpson."

Together, they looked through the emails and other documents on Grayson's computer. Finding a photo wasn't difficult—there were several résumés with his photo, all under different names and with different work and school histories and references. Oddly, they also found social media accounts for those names, all populated with photos of Grayson.

"He's been maintaining multiple identities," Declan said. "He wouldn't have done that for fun. It's likely he uses them for criminal activities."

They found evidence of this theory in his emails. Dessie remembered vaguely that Grayson had once told her he was an investment consultant, and apparently that hadn't been far from the truth.

Only he wasn't so much advising, but rather conning people out of their money. He seemed to use typical pyramid schemes where he gave his clients some return on their investment initially, so they began to trust him and invested even larger sums of money…until they never heard from him again.

He then disappeared and repeated the same con with a different identity elsewhere.

"Maybe he was simply after your money," Declan surmised.

"I don't have any money." Dessie remembered Grayson had been puzzled earlier when she had told him she had no inheritance money to live off. Had he really assumed she was rich?

"Even if he thought I had some extra money in the bank, to set up a long con based on that assumption alone seems like an amateur move. And as we've just discovered, Grayson DuMont is no amateur."

They couldn't figure out what Grayson had hoped to gain from Dessie, but they did put another piece of the puzzle together when they spoke to Charlie Simpson later that afternoon.

"Of course, I know who that is," Connor's uncle said, in reference to the photo they had emailed him earlier. "That's my neighbor's son, Tom Grayson. He was Andrew's best friend. If you ask me, he was a bad influence on Andrew. The two of them were always getting up to no good until Andrew finally dropped him and left for Scotland."

Dessie and Declan exchanged a look.

Tom Grayson and Andrew McKendrick had both assumed other identities—and both had gotten close to Dessie. That could not be a coincidence.

"Is there any chance Tom Grayson intercepted Dessie's first letter, Mr. Simpson?" asked Declan.

Connor's uncle was silent for a moment, but then he conceded, "It's possible. I have a long driveway, and my mailbox is by the street. Tom could have emptied my mailbox without me noticing. I don't know why he would have done that, though. Do you think Andrew was hiding from him and he wanted to find him?"

"Something like that," DI Reid said. "We'll call you when we know more. Thank you, Mr. Simpson."

After they hung up, Declan turned to Dessie and voiced the same question that was on her mind. "Tom Grayson, aka Grayson DuMont, tried to find Andrew—or Connor, as we know him. He heard he had been spotted on Conic Hill. Shortly after, Connor disappears. Afterward, Grayson steals letters sent to Connor's uncle—to keep tabs on what happens with the investigation? What did he have to do with it? And what does he want from you, Dessie?"

CHAPTER TWENTY-FIVE

ANDIE

Andie was even quieter than usual on the drive to Penny's house. She tried to put her personal feelings about Penny aside and just concentrate on how Penny's involvement would help Dessie.

But she didn't succeed. There was something that kept nagging at her.

"Fionna, I didn't want to believe what everyone said about Penny, that she only helps you if it's in her own best interests. But after she unapologetically admitted to selling Grayson the love potion for profit, I think it's true. I have an uneasy feeling about going to her for help, because I'm pretty sure she wouldn't have done it if she hadn't gained something from it. I just can't think what that would be."

Fionna turned bright red, mumbled something under her breath, then said aloud, "It's this turn, isn't it? I rarely drive by myself…"

"Fionna!"

"Okay, okay. I told her I'd owe her a favor if she'd help us."

Andie closed her eyes in dismay. "You didn't have to do that for me. You know what it means to owe her. When she cashes in the favor, you'll have to drop everything and help her, no matter what. Who knows what she'll drag you into? I could have just paid her."

"Yeah, because you're just rolling in cash. I know you don't have any money, Andie. It'll be fine. I can handle myself. By the way, how is the job search going?"

Andie groaned. "Badly. Tarbet Hotel could still be an option if a vacancy comes up, which can happen quickly, I'm told. I'd have better luck if I went back to Edinburgh, but I can't, as long as my real work isn't done here."

Fionna gave her a quick sideways glance before returning her eyes to the road. "You don't have to finish this," she said after a pause. "You gave it a good try. Look after yourself, too. Don't, like, ruin yourself over this. Just ignore your visions and move on. The only thing stopping you is your misguided sense of responsibility."

"Not true. Ignoring my visions is painful. They become more frequent and nightmarish. I don't get any sleep, and sometimes I pass out in the middle of the day. I'm not exaggerating. It's happened to me before. Then there's the guilt if something happens to the person I was supposed to protect." She ran her fingers through her hair. "Oh, I don't expect you to understand. You can choose when to use your ability. It's a gift, not a compulsion. My visions come whether I want them to or not, and I have to live with the consequences."

"My gift has consequences, too," Fionna said quietly.

Surprised by the sad tone in her voice, Andie looked at her friend. "Of course. I'm sorry. I didn't mean to belittle you or your abilities. On the contrary. It's a great gift, with a lot of responsibility attached to it. And you are one of the few people I can imagine doing right by it. Imagine what Penny would do with such an ability. She'd probably cast a spell on her piggy bank so that it would automatically replenish itself with hundred-pound notes."

Fionna grinned. "Good idea. Anyway," she continued, adding a bit of a false cheer to her voice, "my gift is coveted, and that can be useful, too. It gives me the power to get someone like Penny to help us. Your visions are equally magical and important, but it hasn't got as much pull to say, 'In return for your help, I'll promise not to ignore a vision with you in it in the future.'"

On that note, they arrived at Penny's house, parked the car, and got out.

Penny must have heard their voices, as she came out of the garden, a basket full of herbs in her arms. "Hello," she greeted them. "I've already picked the ingredients you mentioned on the phone, Fionna."

Penny acted as if nothing had ever happened between her and Andie, and Andie was fine with that. They had more important things to deal with.

The plan was to start the ritual at sunset. All "in-between times" were considered magical, like transitions between seasons or life and death, or even the liminal dream stage between deep sleep and awakening. Sunrise and sunset were in-between times, too, and thus very conducive to rituals for contacting the spirit world.

It was possible that the ritual would last until after midnight, however. They knew from experience that it could be very exhausting. Once the preparations were finished, they feasted on steak-and-mushroom pie, mashed potatoes, and green beans.

Fionna tried to get a conversation going during dinner but wasn't very successful. The silence grew uncomfortable, but Penny didn't seem to mind.

As they finished their meals, Penny said, "I also made a chocolate cake. Would anyone like a piece? Chocolate helps against stress, and we don't want anyone stressing out during the ritual." Her voice was cheerful, but she shot a meaningful look at Andie.

That was enough to set Andie off. "What I would like to know is why you're suddenly interested in helping Dessie, when you obviously didn't care what happened to her before."

"Andie!" Fionna exclaimed. "We're grateful to Penny for her help, remember? Never mind why. And yes, I'd love a piece of that chocolate cake."

"It's all right," Penny said with a good-natured smile. "And in any case, it's not true that I don't care about what happens to Dessie. On the contrary, I encouraged her to open her heart to love."

"Love for a dodgy and dangerous swindler," Andie blurted out. "You can't tell me you didn't sense something was wrong with this Grayson guy. I sensed it, and with your experience, you should have noticed it, too."

Penny rolled her eyes.

"So, this chocolate cake—" Fionna tried to change the subject, but Andie cut her off.

"I was right in suspecting him, by the way. Tara told me that Grayson had slept with her, but only to get his hands on a key to snoop in the B&B. But that's even worse. It's certainly not the behavior of someone who acts out of pure love."

Penny, who had already gotten up to go to the kitchen, dropped back into her chair. "Really? He slept with that hussy, and he turned me down?" She didn't sound as self-possessed as usual.

"Penny, the cake!" Fionna cried.

Absentmindedly, Penny stood back up. "Yes, of course."

She disappeared into the house and soon returned with a tall cake covered in a thick layer of dark chocolate fondant cream and decorated with chocolate sprinkles. Fionna's eyes grew as big as plates, and Andie could have sworn her friend was drooling a tiny bit.

"That looks good," she had to admit, too.

"Dig in. I've just decided I'd better watch my figure," Penny said.

Interesting, Andie thought, as she licked fondant cream off her fork with relish. Apparently, there was a fair amount of insecurity behind Penny's arrogant demeanor. It made her a smidge more likeable. Still, Andie couldn't forgive her for selling Grayson the love potion, knowing full well that Dessie was in danger. Penny had known about Andie's mission, and loyalty to the other women in the group should always be a priority over personal gain.

After dinner, the sun had moved low on the horizon, and Penny's garden was bathed in a golden light. It was the perfect time to start the ritual.

Fionna lit the candles they had placed in a circle around the fire pit. Penny stoked the small fire and made sure the cauldron with fresh spring water was placed in a good position above it.

Then the three of them took their positions in the circle of candles and began reciting the verses from Fionna's spell book. Penny tossed the herbs into the cauldron in the order they were named.

As they finished chanting, Penny stirred it with a ladle three times counterclockwise and then filled three mugs. Fionna opened her book and read the spell out loud, pausing while they drank the brew, and they continued to recite the spell together.

After a while, they no longer needed the book. The repetition had a meditative effect, and the brew did its job. The three witches no longer had to think about the spell. Words flowed out of their throats as if brought forth by the spirits they were calling upon to help Dessie McKendrick. Their bodies began to move to the rhythm set by the words, and soon they were dancing around the fire.

This wasn't Andie's first experience of a magical trance

state, but it amazed her every time that she managed to turn off her mind and let her body take over. She was stuck in her own head so much, she felt almost ecstatic to let go of her thoughts and trust her senses.

Soon, she didn't even consciously perceive her surroundings anymore. She instinctively knew where the candles, the fire, and the demarcation of the circle were.

Her vision turned inward briefly, then turned outward again with a new focus. Instead of Penny's herb garden, the flames, and the three female figures, she saw energy. Pulsating colors in the spaces where Penny and Fionna were dancing. Little spots of light where animals were present in the garden.

Andie's vision seemed to expand even more. She drifted into the air, higher and higher, until she had a bird's-eye view of Penny's house and garden and then the whole of Tarbet and Arrochar. She could perceive the energy of each person, like colorful bubbles dotted everywhere.

She zoomed in on Dessie's B&B, focusing on the spot of energy in room number three. No, it wasn't just one, but two live energies present. Who was in the room with Dessie?

Before the answer to that question revealed itself , Andie was back in Penny's garden. For a moment, she saw the candles, the cauldron, the other two witches dancing… then she sank to the ground, overwhelmed by a different kind of vision.

Andie couldn't see who she was in her vision, but she knew all the same: Connor McKendrick.

CHAPTER TWENTY-SIX

DESSIE

DI Reid had been reluctant to leave Dessie alone in the B&B, but she couldn't imagine that Grayson would pose any danger to her. "He's not a violent thug or anything like that. We don't know what his aim was, staying here, gaining my confidence all these years, but we have seen how adept he is at taking on new identities. When he figured out his game was up, he didn't hesitate. He cut his losses and hightailed it out of here. He's probably out of the country by now."

Declan wasn't so sure. "That depends on what he was after. He's invested so many years in this con, it might not be something he'll give up that easily."

Dessie couldn't imagine Grayson coming back anytime soon. Still, she promised the inspector she'd lock all the doors and windows. "He did have access to all the keys while I was sick, though. He could have made copies."

"Then you should have the locks changed as soon as possible," Declan advised.

"I'll call a locksmith first thing tomorrow. And I'll sleep in room number three tonight," she decided. "That should be safe. I'm the only one with a key for that room. It's private."

Inspector Reid packed up Grayson's laptop so that his investigators could dig deeper and said his goodbyes. "Hopefully, we'll find out soon what his motive was or get some other evidence for fraud. Then I'll get the resources for a manhunt, and we can find this guy and question him."

Now she lay on the freshly made bed in room number three and regretted trying to put on a brave face in front of the inspector.

The B&B was so dark and quiet, and it unsettled her that she was there all by herself. She almost always had guests. Maybe she should have rented a room somewhere for the night, but that seemed so ridiculous, considering she owned a B&B.

Connor's things in boxes and piles around the room took on an eerie quality in the dark, too, as the shadowy shapes seemed to watch her. Dessie resolved to get rid of everything as soon as possible. For now, all she could do was pull the duvet over her head and focus on counting sheep until she finally fell into a restless sleep.

A noise startled her awake. Her heart started racing, and she held her breath so she could listen.

It sounded like a creaking door.

Dessie bolted upright, pulling down the covers.

The door was halfway open, and in the gap she saw the silhouette of a person, illuminated from the back by a faint light in the corridor.

Dessie opened her mouth to scream, but only a choked sound came out. The person stepped into the room and flipped the light switch.

Dessie blinked into the startling brightness. It took a moment for her brain to process what she was looking at.

Grayson, with a gun in his hand.

"Hello, Dessie," he said with a sneer. "Surprised to see me?"

Dessie shook her head in confusion. Her mouth was dry, but she managed to say, "How did you get in here? Where did you—"

"I've had a key to this room for years," Grayson said smugly. "I've visited your sad little museum before. You didn't even notice, did you? Well, you rarely notice anything that isn't directly related to you. Your useless collection of artifacts and your ridiculous collage weren't of any help to me, either. But the key to this room is coming in handy now." He gave her a nasty grin.

Dessie sat frozen on the bed. Grayson's behavior felt so surreal; she just didn't understand what was going on.

"Well, now it's time to stop the games," Grayson continued, his gun still pointed at her. "I gotta say I'm glad, because I'm getting tired of pretending to like you. Let's try this method, instead: You're going to tell me what you know, or I'll shoot you."

"What…what do you mean, tell you what I know? You mean about Connor's case? I don't know anything, I…" As the shock slowly wore off, Dessie got more and more confused.

Being threatened with a gun felt too unreal for her to be scared. Something like that only happened in movies, didn't it?

Dessie got up and slowly moved toward Grayson. "Did you have anything to do with Connor's disappearance? Tell me, and maybe we can—"

Grayson stopped her in her tracks by letting out a loud and bitter laugh. "What? Then you're going to share?"

"Share? Share what?"

"Stop playing innocent! Andrew gave it to you. He told me. And you're going to tell me where you hid it."

"What...what did he give me?" Dessie cried out desperately.

Grayson seemed to lose his patience. He grabbed her and pushed her out the door. "Come with me!" He pushed the gun into her back and nudged her forward with it. "To the kitchen. We're going through the back. I parked right next to the garden. We don't want the neighbors to over-hear anything and call the police. Although, by the time your pal, the great inspector, gets here, we'll literally be over the hills and far away." Grayson laughed, sounding like he was enjoying himself in his role as the villain.

It was probably a relief for him to be himself and not have to pretend anymore, Dessie thought. "Where are we going? Wait, I don't have shoes on," she said, in an attempt to stall him, as he opened the porch door.

"You don't need them," Grayson said dryly, and pushed her onto the patio.

Dessie shivered in the chilly night air. She was barefoot, wearing only jogging bottoms and a tank top. Following an impulse, she grabbed the plaid Andie had left on the porch swing what felt like an eternity ago.

Pulling it around her, she faced Grayson. "Whatever you think you need to do, you—"

Grayson grabbed her violently by the shoulder, yanked her around, and pushed the barrel of the gun into her back. "Go!" he barked.

Dessie held her breath and walked straight ahead. She barely felt the cold grass under her soles. Her mind was racing, trying to think of a way to get out of this situation, but when Grayson ordered her to climb the narrow fence that separated her garden from the street, she didn't know what else to do but comply.

Grayson held the gun steadily pointed at her as he stepped over the fence with his long legs. Panicked, Dessie looked around, but there was nobody in the street, and before she could call for help, Grayson had already opened the car door and pushed her in.

He quickly got in on the driver's side.

Dessie tried to tell herself that there still might be a chance to flee. Grayson couldn't very well keep his eyes on the road, steer the car, and threaten her with a gun at the same time. Could he?

In the meantime, she would try to reason with him. Whatever had compelled him to do this, there had to be a way to connect with him. She couldn't have been that wrong about him.

"Where are we going?" she asked, trying to keep her voice steady. "If we could just talk this over—"

"Oh, don't worry, I will get you to talk," Grayson said as they drove off, one hand on the steering wheel, the other in his lap, with the gun still pointed at her. It looked effortless, as if he wasn't doing it for the first time.

Americans who drove automatics could steer one-handed and shoot one-handed, Dessie thought, and she knew she was about to lose it.

Get a grip, she told herself.

"The B&B is completely empty, you know," she tried again. "There are no guests. We can talk there without being disturbed, too. No need to drive somewhere else."

"I know how stubborn you are," Grayson said. "How long have you refused to give up on Andrew? For ten years? And how long have you refused to open up to me?" He shook his head in disdain. "Who knows how long it will take to make you tell me where the loot is? It might take days, maybe weeks, but I will thoroughly enjoy torturing you until you do. I have picked a nice, secluded spot for us, where nobody will find us. Where nobody will hear you scream."

CHAPTER TWENTY-SEVEN

ANDIE

Connor woke up to a noise he couldn't identify right away.

He opened one eye. Dessie was snuggled up to him, sleeping blissfully, like an angel. If angels had a habit of snoring. A smile spread across his face.

That sound again. A soft knock. Connor turned his head and squinted. The light coming through the window blinded him, though it was still the soft light of an early Scottish summer morning. He made out the silhouette of a person.

Someone was standing outside the window knocking, he thought sleepily.

But his sleepiness fled when he recognized the face of the person peering through the window above the yellow note warning against midges.

Tom Grayson!

Tom's dark eyebrows were drawn together, and his expression was grim, but triumph gleamed in his blue eyes.

Connor had to hand it to the bastard.

How the hell had he managed to find him on the other side of the world, here, in the middle of a backwater in the

Scottish Highlands? And after he'd changed his name to Connor LaFleur. Damn!

Tom made a hand gesture indicating that Connor should come outside—and quickly. Connor feverishly considered his options.

If he didn't go outside, Tom would probably create a fuss, and Dessie would find out who he really was and what he had done. He had to avoid that at all costs.

He could pretend to go outside to meet Tom and then quickly make a run for it. Tom had always beaten him on the running track in PE, though, and where would he run to? The train station? There was a train every hour, but he probably wouldn't get away before Tom caught up with him. He could try to hide somewhere in Tarbet… But then he'd have the same problem: if he managed to escape, Tom would go after Dessie.

Tom knocked a little louder, obviously annoyed. Connor made a placating gesture and got up carefully. Dessie stirred, and he stayed still with bated breath, but she just mumbled something and settled back into sleep.

Connor quickly put on the pants and T-shirt he had draped over a chair to dry yesterday. He would have liked to slip his feet into his flip-flops, but they were in his backpack, and it would make too much noise to get them out now. He grabbed his hiking shoes with yesterday's socks in them and his wallet before he quietly left the room.

When Connor opened the front door, Tom was already standing there. He must have sprinted around the house to catch him. "Hey, man," Connor said lamely, and sat down on the bench in front of the house to put his socks and shoes on.

"You son of a…," Tom started, but Connor held up his hand. "Shh. Wait until nobody can hear us. I promise, I'll explain everything."

Outwardly calm, his thoughts were racing, trying to

think of something he could say to placate Tom. He couldn't think of any excuses. His pal knew him too well; he wouldn't believe him.

He had double-crossed his best friend and taken off with his share.

He was in deep shit.

But Tom could still forgive him, couldn't he?

They had history.

Connor had saved Tom's ass more times than he could count.

It had started in school, when Connor had taken the fall for Tom for a prank that would have had his friend expelled. Or that time Connor had posed as Tom's lawyer to get him out of jail in some hillbilly town in Alabama. That clueless Podunk sheriff hadn't known what hit him!

Yep, he'd always had Tom's back. Like during that job in Florida, when Tom had tried to talk this old hag at the retirement resort into handing over her dough. The old battle-ax had hardly been able to believe her luck, but she hadn't been shy, oh no! Couldn't keep her wrinkled, liver-spotted hands to herself. And Connor, the good friend that he was, had made sure Tom didn't have to be alone with her. He wondered whether Tom would have gone through with it, if push came to shove. But knowing his pal, he would have shoved the old bat without a qualm to get to her money. He always got what he aimed for, no matter what he had to do.

That's probably how he'd managed to find Connor.

Connor decided he would just admit that he had messed up and remind Tom of the good times.

But Tom wouldn't even hear him out as they walked away from that ugly-ass B&B toward the loch.

"We were partners, man!" he exclaimed. "Since childhood. Us against those idiots we robbed. And then you rob me. Are you out of your mind?"

Connor tried a joke. "Hey, you know damn well it gets addictive. It's not about the money, but about what you can get away with. Maybe I was bored. I needed a challenge. You know, conning the con man who knows all my tricks." He grinned, pulled his pack of cigarettes out of his pocket, and lit one.

Tom gave him a nasty stare. "You're right. I know your tricks. Because you learned them from me. Always put your heart and soul into it. And man, you did that. I wouldn't have thought you'd go that far. Marrying a woman to legit change your identity. That's almost so good it makes up for your stupid idea of going back to your home country."

"No, it wasn't like that, buddy. I didn't marry her just because…"

"I don't care about any of that," Tom interrupted him. "I just want to know where the loot is. Half of it is mine, just in case you've already forgotten, buddy."

They had arrived at the loch by then, and Connor automatically followed Tom as he walked along the shore. They were alone here at this hour, Connor noticed. He could take his time convincing his friend to forgive him. He would give him his share eventually, but he couldn't let him know where it was. Keeping it safe was paramount. For himself and Dessie.

"I don't have it," he answered evasively.

"What's that supposed to mean?" Tom said through clenched teeth.

"Hey, don't get upset, okay? I…lost it."

"Don't give me that shit!" Tom pushed him, and Connor went backward, tripped over a branch on the beach, and fell into the shallow water of Loch Lomond.

"Great, now my ass is wet," he grumbled, trying to get back up.

"Where. Is. It?" Tom stood over him with fists clenched. His face was red.

"I lost it, for real. It was stupid. I'm ashamed to tell you. I celebrated, got shit-faced, and buried the loot. When I woke up the next day with a massive hangover, I couldn't remember where."

His butt was starting to get cold. Connor thought about the pack of cigarettes in his back pocket. Great, they were probably soaked.

"I know when you're lying," Tom yelled. "I can't believe you'd dare lie to my face like that."

Without warning, Tom lunged at him. Stunned, Connor automatically crawled backward, but the ground was suddenly gone under his hands. He flailed his arms, trying to get up, but Tom grabbed him, and Connor lost his balance again.

Unfortunately, his friend had always beaten him at wrestling in school, too, Connor remembered, even though it wasn't the time or place to get nostalgic. Tom meant serious business.

How serious, Connor only realized too late, when Tom pushed his head under the water. Now Connor fought in earnest. He managed to free himself and resurfaced, coughing and spitting water. "Are you nuts, man?"

"Where. Is. It?"

Connor couldn't come up with anything to say, and he hesitated too long. Tom pushed his head underwater again.

The next time Connor freed himself from Tom's grip, he stayed underwater and threw himself toward the nearby shore. But he was too slow. Tom was already behind him and threw himself on top of him.

Connor's cheek pressed against sand and stones. The counterpressure of the ground beneath him meant Connor couldn't slip from his friend's grip. In vain, he tried to twist his head.

After what felt like an eternity to Connor, his lungs bursting and his chest hurting like hell, Tom finally let go.

Connor frantically sucked in air.

"Where is it?"

"Stop it, you lunatic!" Connor finally managed to get out of the water, swiping his wet hair from his face. "I'll tell you, all right? Dessie's got it. I gave it to her. She has my trust. I told her to hide it and not tell me where. So nobody could get it out of me. Really. That's the truth."

"Bullshit! I know you, Andrew McKendrick. You don't trust anyone but yourself. I'm going to ask one last time. Tell me where it is."

"Dessie has... She…"

Before Connor could finish, Tom had pushed his head back under the water. Connor's teeth hit the bottom, and he tasted sand in his mouth. He tried to spit it out, but Tom didn't give him a chance. He kept pushing.

Andrew Connor McKendrick realized too late that his friend would not forgive him this time. The game was up.

CHAPTER TWENTY-EIGHT

DESSIE

essie tried to reason with Grayson, but to no avail. Her panic grew when she understood Grayson was deadly serious. He really wanted to take her somewhere to torture her.

By that time, they had left Tarbet and the populated surrounding area and were well on their way into the Arrochar Alps. Grayson was racing around the curves, and Dessie had to abandon her vague plan to jump out of the car.

Even if she could get out the door before Grayson pulled the trigger, she might injure herself. Then she'd have to get away from him, navigating the uneven terrain in the dark, with no one nearby to help her.

"Listen, I swear, I'd happily tell you everything you want to know, but I don't know what you want from me," she cried out in exasperation.

Dessie looked around frantically, trying to get her bearings. If Grayson slowed down a little, maybe she should just make a run for it. She had to try…

"Sit still!" Grayson turned off the road onto a dirt path.

It seemed familiar to Dessie. "Are we going to the cabin?" she asked in a trembling voice. "The one where the women's group met?"

"Genius, isn't it?" he said smugly. "They won't think of their own secret meeting place when the police ask villagers to help look for you. I reckon I have a couple of days to get the information out of you. I probably won't need that long. It's a shame. I was looking forward to improvising with torture devices."

"I'm telling you, you don't need to torture me at all. I'd tell you what you want to know if I had any idea what you want from me!" Dessie implored.

Grayson hit his hand flat against the steering wheel. "I said, stop playing games with me! Of course you know where the loot is, Andrew told me."

"What…loot…?" Dessie broke off and took a deep breath, trying to calm herself so that she could make sense of what Grayson was accusing her of.

Grayson was after something Connor had had. Money or something else that was valuable. Grayson was convinced that Connor had given it to her. Grayson wanted it. No, his anger and bitterness suggested that he felt entitled to it.

"Connor betrayed you," she said slowly. "He took something that belonged to you."

Grayson snorted. "Goes to show you can't trust anyone, not even your best friend. The bastard ran off with my cut and gave it to his fucking girlfriend. And he thought I was going to let him get away with it! He had it coming!"

Dessie stared at Grayson. "Connor really told you this? That I had the…loot? When?" Her chest felt constricted, and she couldn't breathe. "When exactly did he tell you this, Grayson?"

"What difference does that make? Whatever Connor had, you have it now. That's what happens when you die, isn't it? Everything goes to the spouse." His lips twisted into a hateful grin.

"Why are you talking as if you know he is dead?" Dessie croaked. "You know what happened to him, don't you?"

Grayson's expression changed. It was as if his face had slipped into neutral, no emotions showing at all. His eyes seemed dead when he pulled the car into the small car park that had been full of the women's cars only a few nights ago. It was completely empty now.

Dessie pushed aside the shock of the realization of what had happened to Connor. She couldn't let it immobilize her because this might be her only chance.

Grayson was in a strange trance state, and the car was still.

Dessie made a quick decision, pushed the car door open, and rushed out.

She heard Grayson curse behind her as she made her escape into the woods. She pulled the plaid over her head to shield herself a little from the branches hitting her in the face. Dessie couldn't do anything about her bare feet, but she barely noticed the pain.

She had to focus on not tripping over anything and orienting herself in the pitch dark.

The noise she made while thrashing through the undergrowth, her own panting breath, and the blood rushing in her ears made it impossible to hear whether Grayson was hot on her trail.

But the gunshot was so deafening that she immediately stopped and threw herself onto the ground. She crawled behind a bush and forced herself to calm her breathing and be as still as possible.

She couldn't tell from which direction or how far away the gunshot had come.

Dessie mentally scanned her body, relieved to sense that the bullet hadn't hit her.

She held her breath and listened, but it was dead silent. In the dark, she could see nothing but the outline of trees and bushes.

A second gunshot sounded so close that she was sure she felt the bullet whiz past. An involuntary scream escaped her lips.

"You can't run away from me, Dessie!" she heard Grayson's voice nearby. "I'm going to get you!"

She rushed off in the opposite direction of the voice, running as if the devil himself were after her. She relied completely on her instincts now, like a hunted animal.

Dessie could no longer feel her feet. The plaid hung loosely around her shoulders, and her chest burned, but she couldn't care about any of that.

The trees were thinning and soon wouldn't provide much cover, but with Grayson behind her, Dessie couldn't change direction. Soon she was beyond the tree line, on a grass- and heather-covered slope. At least the moonlight offered a bit of illumination now, and she could see where she was going—toward the edge of a precipice.

Grayson had her cornered!

Panicked, she turned around and held up her hands. "Stop, stop!" she cried, panting. "Grayson, don't shoot, stop!"

Grayson emerged from among the trees, the gun pointed at her.

Dessie automatically backed away. "Please Grayson, I swear to you, I don't know where the loot is, but all of Connor's belongings are in room number three, and if we go back to—"

"I've searched that room several times. The diamonds aren't there. You have until the count of five to tell me where you hid them."

Diamonds?

"I don't have any diamonds!" She sobbed out of desperation. "Don't you think I would live a different life if Connor had given me a fortune? Please, please, think about it. You've checked my financial situation, haven't you?"

"That's how I know you must still have them hidden somewhere," Grayson said.

Dessie thought she heard a hint of uncertainty in his voice, and she clung to that.

"Everything Connor left me is in room number three," Dessie repeated, sounding near hysterical. "He definitely, definitely didn't give me any diamonds."

Grayson seemed to be thinking.

Thank god she was getting through to him. "I don't want any diamonds, especially if they're stolen. Believe me, you're welcome to them!"

Tears were streaming down Dessie's face. "All I want is for Connor to come back...but now I know he won't...I'm leaving Tarbet...Scotland...I don't want anything...you can have everything...everything in room number three...I won't even tell anyone what you did, I just want to forget... I don't care anymore."

Grayson's face hardened. His arm had dropped a few inches, but now it went back up, and he pointed the gun at Dessie again.

"You silly little thing," he said quietly. "Now that you know I'm responsible for Connor's death, I can't let you go, can I?"

Dessie felt a huge pressure against her chest that propelled her backward over the precipice.

Only then did she hear the deafening sound of the gun.

Grass and moss-covered boulders broke her fall—it wasn't that far down. She slid farther down the slope, sharp stones scratching her skin.

At some point she came to a halt, and she just lay there, the dark Highland scenery spinning around her.

As Dessie finally came to her senses, it dawned on her that jumping over the precipice before he shot her might have been her best option. She might have been able to get farther away from Grayson.

But it was too late for that.

A burning sensation spread through her chest. She couldn't manage to get her hand up to touch it, but she was sure it would come away sticky with blood oozing out of the wound.

Dessie couldn't believe this had happened. It seemed completely surreal.

Grayson had shot her.

And this time, the bullet had hit her right in the heart.

CHAPTER TWENTY-NINE

ANDIE

The first thing Andie saw when she opened her eyes again was the orange sky. Confused, she propped herself up on her elbows.

"She's awake!" she heard Fionna say in a squeaky voice.

Andie looked around. She was still in the circle, but the candles had been reduced to burned-down stubs. The campfire was still flickering. Someone had put a pillow under her head and covered her with a warm blanket. Andie's gaze finally found Fionna.

She was on a deck chair on the veranda, wrapped in a blanket herself. It looked as if she'd spent the night there.

Fionna shook the person next to her awake. Penny.

They crawled out from under their blankets and came toward her.

Andie sat up and ran her hands through her hair. "How long was I unconscious?" she asked, looking at the dawn sky.

"Hours!" exclaimed Fionna. "We were so worried about you. We didn't dare take you out of the circle."

"I told her to trust the ritual." Penny yawned. She clearly hadn't worried that much.

"What happened?" Fionna cried. "It was just supposed to be a protection spell for Dessie."

"Yes, who knows what spirits you've awakened with that old book of yours, Fionna," Penny muttered.

"Hey, I researched it, and I was sure—"

"It wasn't Fionna's fault," Andie interrupted the argument. "At least, I don't think it was. I had a vision, and I don't know how much it had to do with the spell." Andie frowned. "It was intense. Different. Usually, I see the double of the person I'm supposed to help. I see a dream version of what happened, not reality. But this time, I saw what happened. Through his eyes. It felt very real. Maybe the spell acted like a catalyst, I don't know…" She shook her head. "It doesn't matter. What's important is that I saw who killed Connor McKendrick. I was there when it happened. I was Connor."

"Who?" Fionna asked. "Who killed him?"

Andie looked up at the two women standing over her. "Grayson."

Penny rolled her eyes. "Well, that's handy, isn't it? I bet now you feel completely justified in vilifying me for helping him."

Andie and Fionna gave her nasty looks before Andie pushed the blanket off and stood up.

"Yes, my instinct was right, and now I know for sure. It was Grayson I was supposed to protect Dessie from." She paused. She felt a little dizzy and put her head in her hands.

Suddenly, she remembered something. Startled, she looked at the others. "What did you see during the ritual? Did you also see life energies like lights and Dessie in her B&B?" The confused looks on their faces confirmed Fionna and Penny didn't know what she was talking about.

"It doesn't matter. Just trust me. I'm pretty sure I saw two people at the B&B in room number three. That can't be good. Come on, we have to go there, quick!"

She was about to storm out of Penny's garden when the blond witch grabbed her arm. "Hang on. We need an actual plan. What if Grayson is still there, threatening Dessie? What are you going to do, march up to him and tell him to stop and turn himself in to the police?"

Andie frowned. She didn't want to admit it, but Penny was right.

"I'll tell you what," Penny continued. "We'll call my brother. He can pick us up, and then we'll go to the B&B together."

Andie had to concur that it was the most sensible thing to do, even if she wanted to get to Dessie as soon as possible. It had been hours since she'd seen the two people in the B&B. Who knew if they were still there—if Grayson was still there.

Besides, the sooner the police learned the truth about Connor's death, the better.

While they impatiently waited for DI Reid to show up, she gave Fionna and Penny a detailed account of what she had seen through Connor's eyes, and they all repeatedly tried to call Dessie—she didn't pick up.

Apparently, Declan had done the same on his way over. "Dessie won't answer her phone," he said, as he got out of his car.

He was clearly very concerned.

"How do you know Grayson is responsible for Connor's death? I just started an investigation into him this afternoon because we found incriminating evidence against him, but we haven't found anything that suggests he killed Connor."

Andie swallowed and looked at Penny. They should have discussed what exactly to tell her brother. Maybe he already knew about their gifts? That would certainly help keep the explanation short.

"You can tell me about it on our way to the B&B," Declan said, already back in the driver's seat. "Andie, sit next to me and explain everything."

The three young women quickly got into Declan's car.

Andie decided not to tell the inspector about the vision. "Look, I just know it was Grayson, okay? You've got to trust me on this. Most importantly, I know where Connor was killed. Maybe we'll find something there, some evidence. We can discuss how I know later, but right now it's more important that we help Dessie and make sure she's safe."

Declan Reid looked in the rearview mirror and met his sister's gaze.

"You're right," he finally said. "This is more important."

Before Declan reached the street with Dessie's B&B, he turned off the headlights. They drove by the house slowly. It was almost daylight out, but they could still see that the lights were on in a few windows of the B&B.

Andie pointed out Grayson's rental car in front of the house.

"And there's Dessie's car," Declan noticed.

"Does that mean we're not too late?" Fionna said excitedly. "They're still in there?"

"Despite being an excellent police officer, my brother probably can't see through the wall," Penny remarked dryly.

"That is true. Which means I need to go in," Declan said. "You guys stay here."

"I'll come with you," Andie said, and was about to open the door. Declan held her back. "It's too dangerous, Andie." He drew his gun as if to make his point.

"You brought your service weapon?" Penny asked, astonished, as it was very unusual.

"Even I have a sixth sense sometimes, Penny," he said, giving her a knowing look.

"I'll come with you," Andie repeated. "I used to work there, and I know how we can get in. What else are you going to do? Ring the doorbell?" She was out of the car before the inspector could stop her. Cursing, Declan got out and rushed after her.

"You show me how to get in, but you stay out of the building," he hissed. "This is a matter for the police. It's my responsibility to keep you out of danger."

Andie just put her finger to her lips and climbed over the garden fence. Declan followed her as she stepped into the flower bed to the right of the patio. The lit windows were on the other side. "The window in this room doesn't close properly. Maybe we can jimmy it open," she whispered.

Declan nodded and looked around as she tried her luck with the window. He put a hand on her shoulder and pointed to the patio door. "No need."

Astonished, Andie noticed that the porch door into the kitchen was ajar.

"Stay out here," Declan warned her one last time, but Andie followed him into the house. She counted on him not wanting to raise his voice and alert anyone of their presence, and she was right. He gave her the evil eye and then ignored her. They tiptoed through the kitchen, and Declan carefully pulled open the door to the hallway, his gun at the ready.

It was dead quiet except for the ticking of the grandfather clock in the hallway. Andy stayed behind Declan but pointed at room number three.

They slowly walked toward the door. The inspector

pressed Andie gently against the wall next to the door, and she understood she was supposed to take cover.

Declan gave the door a very light push. It wasn't locked and opened a crack. He waited, listening, but no sounds came out of the room. Andie caught herself holding her breath.

Declan quickly opened the door, rushed through it with the gun, and called, "Police—turn around and show me your hands."

Andie put her foot in the door so it wouldn't swing shut completely, but she couldn't see anything. Then she heard someone cursing. She recognized the voice.

Grayson!

"Where's Dessie?" Declan asked.

"Wouldn't you like to know?" Grayson sounded far too smug, and Andie's stomach churned with dread.

"You are under arrest for breaking and entering," Declan said in an icy voice. "I'm taking you to the station. If you don't want to make the situation worse for yourself and add abduction to the charges, you'd better tell me where Dessie is."

"I am a guest in this fine establishment. I haven't broken in. You can't arrest me."

"I know for a fact this is a private room, and it is unlawful for you to be here. Besides, you are under investigation for fraud. I can just as easily arrest you for that. You're coming with me. Do yourself a favor and tell me where Dessie is."

Grayson snorted in contempt. "You know what, Detective Inspector, I will come with you. I'm happy to cooperate with the police, even though I've done nothing wrong. You can't pin anything on me, and once we're at the station, I'll call my lawyer. I'm sure he'll advise me not to say anything, so I might as well start taking that advice right now."

Declan didn't reply, but Andie heard a metallic noise. Handcuffs.

"Andie, come in here, please," Declan said.

She slipped into the room. The inspector had handcuffed Grayson, but he was also still aiming his gun at him.

"Take the phone out of my jacket pocket," Declan instructed her. "Press speed dial two and request backup. I have colleagues nearby. They already know what's going on."

Andie's voice trembled, but she managed. As they were waiting for backup to arrive, Grayson stayed quiet. He seemed confident that DI Reid had nothing on him.

Andie had never physically been in the room, but it looked to be complete and utter chaos, nothing like her vision. She couldn't imagine that Dessie had left it in such a state.

Declan drew the same conclusion when he saw Andie looking. "You were searching for something? What?"

Grayson didn't answer.

"Where is Dessie?" Declan sounded angry and looked as if he had to hold himself together not to wipe the smug look off Grayson's face.

Unless Andie was projecting, because she felt the same.

"Andie, have a look around the B&B and see if there's any sign of her."

Andie searched every room, but her feeling that Dessie wasn't there was confirmed.

When the reinforcements arrived, she let them in, and Declan gave his colleagues instructions on how to handle Grayson.

As they were taking the prisoner away, she whispered to Declan, "She's not here."

The inspector ran a hand through his hair. "I have to get Grayson to talk. I wish I could divide myself and look for Dessie, too, but that's not possible. Hopefully, he'll tell

234

us something—maybe I can make him think it's a bargaining chip. Then we'll find her."

He started to follow the other officers out the door, but then he turned around and looked at her imploringly.

"Andie, if you have any idea where Dessie might be… an inkling, you know…I really don't care what it is, and I'm not even going to ask. You'd tell me, right?"

"I would," Andie answered with a sad voice. "But I honestly don't know. I wish I did."

Declan nodded and left.

Andie stared after him.

She didn't know what to do.

She had the distinct feeling that she'd hopelessly failed in her mission to protect Dessie.

CHAPTER THIRTY

DESSIE

Dessie woke up to pain.

Something had scratched her nose.

Her eyes flew open. Yes, her nose hurt, but so did everything else.

Her entire body ached with burning, stinging, and throbbing sensations.

What was happening?

Where was she?

She moved her head and discovered that the culprit for the nose pain was a thistle. In fact, she seemed to be lying in a whole bed of them. It was still dark, but the moonlight radiated from behind the clouds, and the thistles shone in a silvery purple.

Dessie was on her side, one hand tucked under her body. She felt around with the other, stroking the soft woolen fabric of the plaid that still clung to her and then the prickly plants. She found a patch of grass where she could place her hand and pressed herself up into a sitting position.

She immediately regretted the move. Every muscle in

her body reminded her that she had fallen off a rocky outcrop and then rolled down a hill.

Oh yes, after she'd been shot. Automatically, her hand moved to her chest. She expected to feel the worst kind of pain here, but instead she felt…not much of anything. It was sore, like a bruise. Her fingers slipped under the strap of her tank top and felt around where a bullet hole should be.

There was nothing but smooth skin.

Groaning, Dessie stood up carefully. The plaid stayed beneath her feet, a barrier between her soles and the thistles.

She looked around and tried to make out her surroundings.

She was definitely not in her bed and dreaming.

No, she was exactly where she'd remembered ending up. There were grassy hills, heather, and thistles. Even in the darkness, she could make out the overhang she had fallen off, and a little farther, the line of trees Grayson had stepped out of before pointing his gun and shooting her.

Again, her hand went to her chest. She looked down at herself. There was no blood.

Confused, she shook her head. She had heard the shot and felt it. It had catapulted her backward, had caused her to fall over that overhang.

She hadn't imagined that.

Grayson had left her here for dead—but miraculously, she hadn't died.

Suddenly scared that Grayson might still be around, she knew she had to get out of the open as soon as possible.

She took a step onto a patch of grass. The slightly dewy, cold blades felt good under her sore feet.

Dessie picked up the plaid. Unlike her jogging bottoms

and tank top, it had survived the tumble pretty well. In fact, she couldn't see any damage at all.

Pulling the warm plaid around her shoulders, she couldn't help but remember Andie's words when she had given it to her.

Hadn't she said something about a protection spell… that the plaid was supposed to protect her?

No. Not possible. Woolen fabric couldn't act as a Kevlar vest and stop a bullet.

There had to be another explanation for how she had survived.

As she took a few steps down the slope, she also realized how lucky she had been not to have hurt herself worse during the fall. Yes, everything hurt, and she had a lot of scratches and bruises, but there were no broken bones, no twisted ankles.

Dessie kept her eyes on the ground so as to not step on a thistle and finally made it down the slope. There were more trees, and it was darker down here, but she knew she had to pass through the woods and go farther down to get to a populated area.

The most important thing now was to get to a house and have someone get her to the hospital where she could be properly checked out.

Dessie tried to keep her confidence up, but soon fear crept in. She couldn't even find a footpath, let alone a dwelling.

She had no sense of time but was sure she had been wandering around the forest for hours. She became so exhausted that she didn't feel any pain in her body anymore. At first, she thought it was a blessing, but she soon realized it was the pain that had kept her going.

Being numb did her no good. She was dangerously close to giving up.

Those large moss-covered stones started to look really

comfortable. If she could just lay her weary head down and rest a little…

No, she had to move on.

She focused on her fear to sharpen her senses.

There was plenty in the dark forest that scared her.

Invisible animals were making all kinds of noises—or could it be Grayson who had been following her all along, making this a sick game of hunter and prey?

But soon, even her fear wasn't enough to keep her alert. Everything became dull, slightly blurry. She no longer smelled the pine needles, hardly winced when the trees creaked eerily in the wind.

She began to move like a sleepwalker.

Dessie figured the bullet had hit her after all.

Maybe she was, in fact, dead.

Maybe she couldn't get out of these woods because there was nothing else. The deserted Highlands were her own personal purgatory.

Maybe this was hell.

Had she brought this on herself? She had done everything in her power to avoid getting close to others in the last ten years. She had turned down all offers of friendship.

She hadn't lived her life, but instead had wasted all those years. All the opportunities she had been given in life she had squandered. She'd thrown away her dreams. Friends, like Amy, discarded.

For what? What difference did it make if Connor was dead or just gone? He wasn't there anymore. He was no longer part of her life. She had an obligation to go on living without him.

No, she corrected herself, not anymore.

Now it was too late, wasn't it?

She was dead, and her punishment was to wander around this remote Highland hell for eternity, all alone.

Suddenly, a red streak on the horizon captured her

attention. The sun rises in the east, she thought. She had no clue where in relation to "east" she was and what lay in "the east," but it was a direction, at least. Something to move toward.

If this wasn't her personal hell, the fact that she hadn't come across another person might be explained by unintentionally wandering around in circles.

She was rewarded for clinging to this red streak of hope when she stumbled across a path.

Dessie was almost tempted to kiss the dirt, but she feared she wouldn't be able to get back up. Tears were streaming down her face as she followed the path toward the rising sun. She was crying out of relief, but also because of the pain that had returned with a vengeance.

She was no longer numb, and every small injury made itself known. Muscles she never knew she had were incredibly sore, and the soles of her feet felt like open wounds. Scrapes all over her body burned, and dark bruises had formed everywhere.

Just when she thought she couldn't bear it any longer, a cat came into her view on the path in front of her. The brown tabby was big, with long hair, a bushy tail, and funny tufted ears. It looked at Dessie and then turned its head and walked on, as if to say, "Come on, now."

Dessie followed the cat, keeping her eyes on its bushy tail, and almost didn't notice the row of houses that appeared at the end of the path.

She couldn't believe her eyes when she recognized the first one to her left.

The Thistle Inn.

She had arrived in Tarbet.

That was impossible. There was no way she could have walked from near the cabin in the Arrochar Alps to Tarbet in the space of a couple of hours in her condition.

Then again, it was just as absurd as a bulletproof woolen plaid.

The cat sat in Mrs. MacDonald's garden and meowed at her.

Dessie surrendered to the spell and let her feet carry her over the fence into Mrs. MacDonald's garden, around the house, to the front door.

She didn't have the strength to raise her arm and knock, but Mrs. MacDonald opened the door anyway.

"Come in," the old woman said. "I've been waiting for you."

Dessie followed her into the kitchen without saying a word.

Mrs. MacDonald pointed to a chair with an enamel basin on the floor in front of it. The basin was filled with water and what looked like plant debris.

"Sit down and put your feet in there."

Dessie obeyed.

Mrs. MacDonald took the whistling kettle from the stove and poured boiling water into the teapot on the table. Then she draped a blanket around Dessie's shoulders. "Now let's get you warm."

Dessie wanted to scream when she put her feet in the water, it hurt so much. But miraculously, the pain quickly subsided, and the concoction started to feel soothing.

Mrs. MacDonald scooped three spoonfuls of sugar into a cup and poured in the steeped tea. She put the cup in front of Dessie, together with a plate of three lemon wedges.

Dessie wondered how Mrs. MacDonald knew she drank her tea with lemon instead of milk, but compared to everything else, this seemed like a small peculiarity.

Her fingers trembled when she took the cup in both hands and carefully sipped the invigorating brew.

The cup still warming her hands, Dessie looked up at Mrs. MacDonald.

"You had nothing to do with Connor's disappearance. But you knew he was dead all along, didn't you?"

The old lady just nodded. It could have made Dessie angry, but a sense of inner peace had taken hold of her. "Why didn't you tell me?"

"It wasn't up to me to convince you. I know a lot of things about many people. I can't tell them. They have to learn these things by themselves, when the time is right. Even if I could spare them a lot of pain—I can't take that journey away from them. That was my most painful lesson to learn."

A shadow passed over Mrs. MacDonald's face, and for the first time, Dessie saw not just a caricature of an eccentric old lady, but a human being. Mrs. MacDonald looked much, much younger in that instant, except for her eyes.

Dessie averted her eyes and focused on her tea. "Ten years. Ten years I've been looking for Connor. Ten wasted years."

"They weren't wasted." Mrs. MacDonald smiled mysteriously. "They may have been painful, empty, and lonely, but they led you to now. Which is where you're meant to be."

Dessie said nothing to that.

After she finished her tea, she called DI Reid. It wasn't long before his car pulled up in front of the Thistle Inn. Mrs. MacDonald had dried Dessie's feet with a towel and given her a pair of thick wool socks.

Dessie thanked her and was about to leave when Mrs. MacDonald held her back. "You thought you had lost Connor, but he was with you the whole time. You were just looking for what you already had. Now you have to let him go. Then you'll be free to move on, too."

Dessie nodded. Mrs. MacDonald smiled. She again

looked much younger than her years, but the impression lasted only a few seconds. "Now there's space for someone else in your life."

"Oh," Dessie said, embarrassed. "I can't think about a relationship now, after everything that's happened."

"Not with a person, no." Mrs. MacDonald asked Dessie to wait a moment longer. She soon came back holding a small kitten. It looked similar to the cat that had led Dessie the last few hundred yards to Mrs. MacDonald's house.

Dessie carefully touched the tiny tufted ears. "It's a Maine Coon, a sixteen-week-old female. She's looking for a home. I know you're the right person for her."

All kinds of logical objections were at the tip of Dessie's tongue, but for some reason, all she said was, "Okay. Thank you."

CHAPTER THIRTY-ONE

ANDIE

A few days later, Andie and Dessie met DI Reid on the shore of Loch Lomond. A small section of the beach was cordoned off, and two uniformed police officers stood in front of the flapping yellow tape while others were busy searching the area.

A few feet away, a small boat served as a base for the divers, searching for Connor McKendrick's body at the bottom of the loch.

It had taken a bit of extra work to get proper approval for the search. Declan may have believed Andie when she'd said this was the scene of the crime, but he couldn't put "vision" on the form when requesting expensive police resources.

There had been another ritual, this time properly conducted by Mrs. MacDonald, and Andie had been able to point DI Reid to a hollowed out tree under which the remains of Connor's belongings were buried.

Any identifying clothing had long since rotted away, with the exception of part of the soles of his hiking boots. They had struck gold, however, with a very special find. Connor's silver Zippo lighter had been a present from

Dessie. She had purchased it in Glasgow, right after the wedding, and it had their wedding date engraved on it.

The find justified employing the divers—they didn't need to know that DI Reid had received very specific information about Connor's remains. In another vision, Andie had seen Grayson removing the spare tire from his rental car, chaining Connor to it, and dragging his body into the loch. The tire would have sunk to the bottom.

Connor's body would have decomposed and disintegrated, and it would likely have dislodged from the chains. Grayson had been lucky that no body parts had turned up on the shore of the loch. But they only needed one speck of DNA attached to the tire. They could compare the DNA with a sample from Connor's uncle, and the tire could link Tom Grayson to the rental car he had paid for with one of his known aliases ten years ago.

It seemed that the divers had found the tire, or at least a tire, and DI Reid had called Dessie to come over to the search site.

Andie, who was back working at Dessie's B&B, had been keen to accompany her.

Now they waited with bated breath until someone on the boat spoke to the inspector on his walkie-talkie.

"The serial number matches the missing rental car tire," Declan repeated, though the two women had already heard.

Andie exhaled in relief. "That's good. But that's just… circumstantial evidence, right? If there's only the car tire and Connor's lighter? If they don't find anything else?"

Declan looked at Dessie with concern.

"It's okay," Dessie said with a brittle smile. "You can tell us. They found his body, didn't they?"

DI Reid sighed. "So far, they've found a couple of long bones and a skull. If they belong to Andrew Connor McKendrick, we'll know soon."

Dessie nodded. There was no hope in her eyes, just acceptance. The DNA test wasn't necessary for her to confirm what she already knew.

Connor was dead.

"Is this enough to put Grayson behind bars?" she asked skeptically.

"Andie's right. It's all circumstantial evidence. There are no witnesses to the murder." He glanced at Andie. "At least none whose testimony would mean anything in a court of law. And it is very unlikely we'll find DNA or fingerprint evidence linking Grayson to the scene of the crime after all these years. But we are building a case against Grayson. He has stalked you for years, Dessie, kidnapped you, and made an attempt on your life. He can't talk himself out of that. And then there's all the evidence of his con jobs. Being cheated out of the money from a con job seems like a good motive, and considering he had that heavy chain and something like a spade in his rental car, it makes it look like the murder was premeditated. Grayson might still plead manslaughter, though."

"I don't know if he planned the murder, but he was prepared for it," Andie said. "He was willing to go to extremes to get the diamonds."

Dessie gave a sad sigh. "Those diamonds must have been worth a lot if Connor was prepared to sever ties with his best friend and partner forever, and Grayson went even further and killed his best friend and partner for them."

She broke off with a faraway look in her eyes. Dessie was clearly still processing all the things she hadn't known about her husband, maybe had never wanted to know.

Dessie had confided in Andie that, even more painful than coming to terms with the fact that Connor was dead, there was a possibility that he had never even loved her. That he had married her for convenience, to take on a new identity.

"They were," Declan said softly.

Dessie looked at him in surprise. "The diamonds? You know where they came from? What con job Grayson and Connor had pulled?"

Declan nodded. "Thanks to the information we got from Grayson's laptop, we could tie the two of them to a few thefts. The victims who filed reports identified both men when they were shown photos. It became apparent that their scams followed a certain pattern. One of them, usually Connor, seduced a rich woman and became her trusted confidant. He bided his time until the topic of an investment or a sale would come up. Connor would then suggest a trustworthy acquaintance who would be just the right person to handle it."

"Let me guess. That trustworthy person would be Grayson," Dessie said cynically.

"Exactly. Grayson would handle the sale or the investment, and the poor woman would never see the profit. Before she knew what was going on, the partners in crime would be gone, busy with a similar scam elsewhere, with different identities."

"And in this case, they ripped off a woman by pretending to sell her diamonds?" Andie asked curiously.

"Yep," Declan said. "And the roles were reversed. Grayson gained the trust of an elderly South African widow who had inherited a diamond mine from her late husband. The woman wasn't interested in continuing to run the business, mainly because she didn't know how to run a business at all, and Grayson convinced her to divest herself of her stock quickly by selling diamonds directly to customers in the US without middlemen. She was taken in by the idea of quick cash—more than enough to live in luxury for the rest of her remaining years—without much work.

Grayson introduced her to McKendrick, who supposedly had the contacts in the US. He picked up the diamonds in South Africa, smuggled them through Customs, and sold them in the States. They stuck to their usual modus operandi by selling a few diamonds and giving the widow a good return on their first trip.

The second time around, the widow stupidly entrusted McKendrick with millions of dollars' worth of diamonds. The woman reported the diamonds stolen but left out the details of the theft. We came across this case, and my colleagues in SA pressured her a bit until she admitted the truth."

Dessie shook her head in disbelief. Andie could guess what she was thinking. It sounded like a plot from a movie. It seemed absurd that two people who had been in their lives, Connor and Grayson, had actually pulled off such a con. Granted, Andie only knew Connor from her vision. It had to be much worse for Dessie, who had been taken in by him, too. She had been as much of a victim as the South African widow. Worse, because Dessie had believed in him and had sought justice for a person who hadn't been real, in a way.

"So Connor couldn't resist the temptation," Dessie said with a bitter voice. "He ran off with the diamonds. Grayson, furious, had his eyes and ears open, finally received a tip from an acquaintance, and wasted no time in coming to Scotland to make Connor pay. Right here."

She looked over to the boat, at the divers searching for Connor's remains.

"You really found out a lot in the last few days," Andie said, impressed. "You must have been working around the clock."

The dark circles under Declan's eyes confirmed he had worked tirelessly on this case and barely slept at all. "It's important that we gather all the evidence we can to build a case against Tom Grayson, and quickly. I will not let him walk again. I want him out of your life, Dessie."

Dessie smiled gratefully at him.

Declan's brows drew together. "What would really tie the case together: finding the diamonds. So far, all we have is the widow's testimony identifying Grayson and McKendrick. But Grayson's motive would be so much clearer if Connor actually had the diamonds."

Dessie just shrugged. "I don't know where they could be. Grayson seemed to be convinced that Connor had given them to me. He believed my husband trusted me. But he was wrong." She sounded so sad. "Connor was a stranger to me."

"Grayson really believed this," Andie said, suddenly very alert. "Connor told him you have the diamonds."

"Maybe only because he wanted Grayson to back off. He was desperate and would have said anything to save himself. He probably sounded convincing. Connor was an excellent liar." Tears sprang to Dessie's eyes.

Andie put her arm around the taller woman's waist. "I'm sorry. "

"It's okay," Dessie said, wiping her eyes. She took a shaky breath. "Hey, remember you said you'd help me get rid of Connor's things? Let's do that now. I think it would help me. I've been ready to do it for a while, and today…" She looked at the boat. "Having found out what happened to him…having found him…it seems like it's time."

Andie nodded. "Of course. Let's do it."

Dessie turned to Declan. "Thank you. For going above and beyond, for calling us to witness this…I am so grateful. All of this helps me get closure."

"Of course. And Dessie…" Declan touched her lightly on the arm. "I'm going to do everything I can to put Grayson behind bars. I mean it. Your safety, your happiness, are important to me."

Andie had the feeling she was intruding on a very private conversation. She hoped Dessie wasn't too preoccupied with Connor to notice that Declan wasn't talking to her as a police officer.

But Dessie's smile confirmed to Andie that she understood the nature of Declan's feelings.

DI Reid was a good man, Andie thought. She hoped that in time Dessie could open up to the possibility of a new relationship.

They headed back to Dessie's B&B.

The kitten, who Dessie had named Nova, was waiting at home for them. She didn't like to be alone, so Dessie brought Nova into her room at night and into the breakfast room during the day. She tried to remember to ask guests if they were allergic, but so far, everyone had enjoyed the company of the little furball. None of the guests were around right now, though, so Dessie and Andie spent some time playing with Nova before they got on with their work.

Most of what had been in room number three was already packed in boxes and garbage bags. Andie and Dessie looked through what could still be donated, marked those boxes, and loaded them into Dessie's car. They also hauled off the old drink cart; Dessie decided to keep the desk and dresser in the room.

They dropped everything off at a charity shop in Helensburgh and returned for the garbage bags and boxes. Once those were stowed in the car, they stopped for a break.

"Let's have a cup of tea," Dessie suggested.

In the kitchen, sitting at a table with tea and biscuits, Andie asked, "What's going to happen with the B&B?"

"Why?" Dessie smiled and stroked Nova, who was sitting on her lap. "Is this your way of asking if you'll still have a job here next summer?"

"That, too. But I'm also curious about your plans. The

B&B was a means to an end, wasn't it? It enabled you to stay in Tarbet, keep looking for Connor. I wondered if you wanted to return to your old life. What did you do before you moved here?"

"I was in the middle of a drama degree in Canterbury. I met Connor during the Edinburgh Fringe one summer. We had a long-distance relationship for a year and got married on a whim."

"So you wanted to be an actress?" Andie's eyes widened.

"Can't imagine that, can you?" Dessie had to laugh.

Andie made a noncommittal sound.

"That's all right, I get it. I was a different person then. But yes, my dream was to be an actress. I wasn't half bad, either."

"Wow. Okay. And now? Are you going to finish your degree? Get back to acting?"

Dessie sighed. "I haven't considered that, no."

"Why not? You're free now." Andie tried to sound encouraging.

Dessie looked out the window, but her eyes glazed over, as if she didn't see the garden at all. After a moment, she said softly. "Technically, I'm free to do what I want. But we're never completely free of our past…and I'm not the Dessie I was back then. I can't go back in time. That doesn't have to be a sad or even a bad thing. I need to figure out what my life without Connor looks like. I need to discover what's next for me. That's kind of exciting." Dessie shrugged. "For now, I'll keep the B&B. I'll stay here. I might not have imagined this would be my home, but it is. So there will be a job for you here for the foreseeable future."

"Cheers to that," Andie said, raising her teacup. "Hmm. Interesting how relieved I feel. I guess my story is similar, in a way. Before this summer, I wasn't even sure if

I'd ever return to Tarbet. I certainly planned on getting a summer job in Edinburgh. And then this happened. I might not like it much, but I belong here. I'd love to come back and work for you during the busy seasons, when you need me."

Dessie smiled and leaned forward to clink cups with Andie.

"Let's get back to it," she said, after they had finished their tea. "Now that we've talked about it, I can't wait for the next chapter in my life to begin."

They drove the trash to the landfill and returned to clean room number three.

Andie went to fetch the vacuum cleaner, and when she brought it into the room, Dessie was standing next to the bed looking at the few items they had left.

"Do you plan to keep them? Or sell them?" Andie asked, pointing at the silver letter opener and the crystal decanter.

"Sell them. Not sure about the music box, though."

Andie touched the top. "Hang on," she said. "That looks familiar."

"Ugh, it was Connor's wedding gift to me," Dessie explained. "It's probably foolish of me to be sentimental, but for some reason, I can't quite part with it. Connor claimed it had belonged to his mother, and that it was valuable. But it's probably junk." Anger had crept into her voice. "Like all the other things I kept. I thought they were valuable pieces of a puzzle, vital clues that could tell me more about him and what happened to him. I collected these things because I thought they would be able to tell me what happened to Connor. In fact, they didn't even add up to one true life story. It was all lies."

Andie picked up the music box and tried to turn the key to wind it.

"It doesn't even work anymore," Dessie said, no longer

angry or disappointed, but rather deflated. "It used to play circus music, and the animals went around in a circle. But it stopped working right after Connor gave it to me."

Andie inspected the tin circus animals painted with faded colors and the round metal tube in the middle. "It does look old. Look, parts of it are rusted."

"Like I said, it's probably just junk," Dessie said again. "Let's throw it away."

"Wait a minute," Andie said, turning the music box over. There were tiny screws. She assumed you could open it up and pull out the drum with the pins that produced the music. It had to be inside the round tube. There were scratches on the old, darkened metal, as if someone had opened it before. "Do you have a very small screwdriver or a pocketknife?"

Dessie left and returned a moment later with a pock-etknife. It took a while for Andie to remove the tiny screws. The bottom came off, and Andie carefully put two fingers inside. Her eyes widened when she pulled out a velvet pouch.

Dessie looked at her in surprise.

With trembling fingers, Dessie picked up the pouch and pried it open. She shook out some of the contents into her other hand.

"The diamonds," she breathed.

Andie stared in disbelief at the sparkling stones. "So you really did have them all this time. Connor hadn't lied."

"Maybe our life together wasn't a lie, after all." Dessie sounded as if she didn't quite believe what she was saying. Then her eyes narrowed, and she looked at Andie, askance. "Did you know they were here all along?"

Andie shook her head. "No, I swear. I just remembered seeing the music box in a vision. The first one I had of you. I knew you were in danger and that I had to protect you. I didn't even have an inkling about Grayson. I didn't understand what this room meant. And I certainly didn't know about the diamonds or that they were in the music box."

Dessie nodded, put the diamonds back into the little bag, and pulled her phone out of her pocket to call Declan.

"I knew, though," Andie admitted with a mischievous grin, "that you'd speak to Declan Reid again and have a good excuse to meet up with him."

"Then it's not always murder and bad fortune? Sometimes you see good things in your visions?" Dessie asked with hope in her eyes as she waited for Declan to pick up.

"Yes," Andie said, even though she didn't need a vision to see what the future might hold for those two. "Sometimes I get to see beautiful things."

AFTERWORD

Thank you for reading THE WITCH CLUB. I hope you enjoyed reading it as much as I loved writing it. If you did, I would greatly appreciate a review on Amazon or your favorite store or book review site. Reviews are crucial for authors as well as for readers who are looking for their next book—even just a line or two are so helpful. Thanks!

I love to chat with my readers, so if you'd like to contact me, visit felicitygreenauthor.com.

Do you want to know what's next for the SCOTTISH WITCHES? Read book 2 in the series: HERB WITCH FOR HIRE.

If you would like to know more about the other books in the SCOTTISH WITCHES MYSTERY series, get information on latest releases, and receive a free book, please sign up for my newsletter on felicitygreenauthor.com.

Happy reading!
Felicity Green

Printed in Great Britain
by Amazon

42908849R00148